KEP
WESTGUARD
REBEL SPY

Books By Eileen Schnabel

ONE IF BY LAND, TWO IF BY SUBMARINE

KEP WESTGUARD REBEL SPY

WESTGUARD REBEL SPY

EILEEN SCHNABEL

Wonder Jumps Press

ISBN: 978-1-7338681-2-9 (paperback)

ISBN: 978-1-7338681-4-3 (ebook)

www.eileenschnabel.com

Praise for Eileen Schnabel's
ONE IF BY LAND, TWO IF BY SUBMARINE

"Rambunctious YA educational entertainment that reimagines the American Revolution as a time-travel escapade.

—Kirkus Reviews

"A deftly crafted and simply riveting read from first page to last, Eileen Schnabel's "One If By Land, Two If By Submarine" is an extraordinary science fiction story by an author with a genuine flair for originality and a remarkably effective narrative storytelling style...this first volume of a planned series is especially and unreservedly recommended for both school and community library Science Fiction & Fantasy collections for young readers.

—Midwest Book Review

'A page-turning read for any age...recommended to anyone interested in time travel or Revolutionary War events'

—Hidden Histories

Action-packed, Eileen Schnabel captures our imagination and runs with it. Well written, the plot is executed beautifully with finesse and charm. One cannot help but fall in love with the kids and smile with the fresh take on Hancock and Adams. It is a fresh way to look at time travel and the intrigue was fascinating. The characters were very well developed, each character was realistic and her attention to detail made the story unforgettable. Well written with realistic dialog and interactions, it is an easy listen.

—*ACX Review*

Teachers in our school district are always on the lookout for more historical fiction books that correlate with their history unit and this one will definitely be popular with our explorers, and the discovery of America.

—*Goodreads Review*

One If By Land is a fun and educational read. I plan on gifting this book to my nieces and nephews.

—*Amazon Review*

"Those who expect to reap the blessings of freedom, must...undergo the fatigues of supporting it."

—**Thomas Paine**

Dear readers:

Thank you for taking this journey to Saratoga, 1777 with me. Whether you read these pages traveling on the morning school bus, on your way to basketball practice, in study hall or heading to bed at the end of the day, a time travel adventure awaits.

Throughout this series, you will meet historic characters who shaped the world we now live in. The American Revolution was a war against a superpower. In the 1700s, The British had the most powerful military in the world. In contrast, the Continental army was small, untrained, and largely unpaid. Many scoffed that the Americans would even consider challenging the British empire. Across the globe, it was widely believed the rebellion would be quickly squashed.

But the desire for freedom convinced an outgunned, outnumbered group of rebels to fight until they achieved a new country, a new democracy. Many agreed with American Patrick Henry: "Give me liberty or give me death."

History is the biggest adventure story of all time! I hope you enjoy reading these pages as much as I enjoyed writing them.

Kind regards,

Eileen Schnabel

The Saratoga series is dedicated to:

The world's citizens, young and old, who see liberty not as a guarantee, but a responsibility that requires constant effort, thought, and solutions.

My grandpa, who fought with the United States Navy during World War II, to ensure freedom would pass from his generation to future generations.

CONTENTS

Prologue

Call of Duty

The cell phone hidden on the bedroom bookcase vibrated at 11:00 p.m. 13-year-old Kep Westguard lunged toward the bookcase, knocking his Spanish notes off his desk.

He glanced at his closed door, pushed aside swim trophies, grabbed the phone, and read the text.

Mission is a go.

Kep's thumbs jammed his response. *Agree to my terms?*

Dots told him his boss was typing, then nothing. She must have erased it. More dots.

The phone vibrated again. *It's a rash, risky decision to travel there alone.*

He didn't bother to respond. She wasn't telling him anything he didn't know.

For once he had the upper hand with his boss. He was sticking with his decision. He waited for her next message.

Terms accepted.

Kep blew out a sigh and quickly typed. *Cover story as planned?*

Confirmed. 0800 departure.

After carefully sliding the phone back into its hiding place, he gathered up the scattered Spanish notes and stuffed them into a folder. Then he opened his laptop and pulled up the file: SARATOGA BATTLE 1777 MISSION NOTES. Studying for school would have to wait. Conjugating Spanish verbs wasn't going to keep him alive.

Chapter 1

Reconnaissance Mission

The alarm buzzed at 6 a.m. the following morning. This was going to be no typical Saturday. Kep hadn't slept since his boss Annie had texted him. He'd spent the night in front of his computer screen, cramming in specifics about the areas around the Battle of Saratoga and the locations of both the Continental and British armies.

The night before, success on the mission seemed possible, even probable. But his confidence slipped as his alarm clock's red numbers counted down to departure. Maps jumbled in his head. Would he remember the key details?

Doubts began their creepy crawlies right back into his mind.

He forced himself to focus on the computer screen, clicking the keyboard's down arrow again and again. His head was busting with KHM—key historic moments—around the battle.

If his time-traveling, crackpot Grandpa Fox *had* disrupted the timelines, changed any KHMs and tipped the key battle of Saratoga in the Brit's favor, then they could talk about sending the entire team.

His boss Annie, or likely her crew at KRONOS, had created the mission notes and emailed the encrypted file. It wasn't the first time Kep had studied the material. He wasn't like his brilliant brother Max, a national history scholar who seemed to learn this history stuff by osmosis.

Many nights, Kep had pored over the maps and graphs, names and dates. He'd known the call might come, and if it did, he needed to understand the exact history of the battle to know if Fox had changed history.

At 7:30 a.m. Kep closed the computer file, pulled on his *MADISON WEST SWIM* sweatshirt, and grabbed his swim bag. A poster of Olympic champion Michael Phelps wearing all his gold medals urged VISUALIZE SUCCESS. For today, that meant Kep outsmarting the British. The closest thing he'd see to a pool in 1777 New York would be the Hudson River.

He glanced at a framed photo on the shelf next to the poster. Tela, TJ, Max, and Kep. Not his swim team. His other team, his time-travel team. The picture had been taken at Camp Liberty with everyone dressed in their 18th century clothing right before their first time-travel mission last summer. TJ had snapped the picture with his mini–Pocket Popper camera, the same camera that later saved his life in a Boston Jail in 1775.

Kep tucked the photo into his swim bag. Ridiculous, but it kind of felt like they were coming with him that way, at least for the first part of the journey.

He waited for the back door to slam as Mom headed out for her morning class. Kep felt a twang of guilt. All those years in an orphanage with mom thinking she had no living relatives, then to find her family closet held quite the pair of skeletons—namely Annie and Fox. At least Annie could be considered a patriot. In a way, she was like his grandpa on his dad's side, Grandpa Westguard, who'd spent his life in the Navy protecting the U.S. Fox was the fork in the family tree, busy doing everything in his power to destroy it.

Kep passed his little brother's room on tiptoe. If Max knew he was being left behind, he'd be furious. Fortunately, his brother had a chess tournament today, so hopefully, he'd be too busy to suspect another time travel mission was about to start.

Kep softly jogged down the steps to the kitchen.

Play this carefully! If Dad suspected for a second that Kep was meeting his great-aunt Annie, he wouldn't be leaving the house. And the country could end up doomed.

Coffee brewed in a pot on the counter and the room smelled like cinnamon. Dad stirred a pan of bubbling oatmeal with one hand and read a physics book with the other. Only two of the gas burners still worked, but new stoves were expensive and theoretical time travel professors weren't in high demand, so money was tight. Kep suspected Annie, who had to have gazillions of dollars to build a time-travel facility, would be more than willing to lend the family some cash, but her name was mud in their house. Even if they were living in a tent, his parents wouldn't take a dime from her.

Kep tried for the casual just-heading-out-the-door-for-a-swim-meet tone. "Hey, Dad."

His dad looked over. "Your coach's message was a bit garbled, but it sounds like you're heading to scout the competition at a meet up north?"

Kep's coach hadn't left the message, but considering Annie had a team at KRONOS with the technical skills to send people through time, digitally reproducing his coach's voice for a voice mail probably wasn't too difficult.

"Yeah. It came up at the last minute." Kep looked at the worn linoleum as if inspecting whether he'd done a good job mopping, his weekly chore. "It's a long drive and we'll stop somewhere on the way home to eat, so we'll get back really late." Actually, Kep would spend the day snooping around a British encampment nearly 250 years in the past. He wouldn't be ordering french-fries at a McDonald's drive-thru. He'd be lucky to get a tooth-cracking hardtack biscuit at some friendly Redcoat's campfire if he wasn't captured as a spy before the food was served up. "Tell Mom not to wait up."

Kep didn't like lying. And this was bigger than a white lie. Call it a red, white, and blue lie. But considering within a few hours he'd be spying for the rebellion, he might as well get used to it. Spies weren't exactly known for honest answers.

The timing would be tricky. To 1777 and back in about 16 hours. But there was no way he could be gone longer and not raise a lot of red flags.

"A bowl of oatmeal to fuel your day?" asked Dad.

Too nervous to eat, Kep shook his head. "Thanks, but I packed a couple apples and a sandwich."

Call it misinformation. That felt better than lying.

"Want a ride to the school?" Dad pushed up the glasses slipping down his nose. "I'm heading to the library. I could drop you on the way."

"I'll just take my bike." Kep eased toward the door, wishing he could hug his dad. A mission to the Revolutionary War, even a reconnaissance mission, carried risks. As in might-never-return risks. But he had to go on the mission because if Fox changed history, if the trajectory of time changed, there might be no home and no family to return to. His gut squeezed. At 13, he didn't usually hug his parents except for big events, so Dad would likely start asking questions.

When Kep opened the door, Piper dashed over, tail wagging.

"Sorry, Piper." He scratched her favorite spot just behind her ears. "I'll walk you tomorrow. I promise." He ignored the voice in his head that said it was a promise he had no business making.

Dad turned off the stove. "Good luck with your scouting mission."

Kep did a doubletake at the term *scouting mission*, but Dad simply scooped oatmeal into a bowl and settled at the table.

"Thanks."

I'll need a wagonload of it.

Kep quickly biked to the school. An American flag clanked against a flagpole near the bike rack. Kep rolled his front tire into the rack and clicked the lock into place. At least he hadn't lied about his first destination.

Moments later, a black sedan with tinted windows drove into the deserted school parking lot and slowed to a stop.

When Kep saw the driver was Mule, a familiar face from Kep's first time travel mission, he felt a little less nervous. He opened the back door and tossed his bag onto the seat.

"Heard you ditched your teammates," said Mule.

"I didn't *ditch* them," said Kep. "I'm just taking care of this mission myself."

"You never learned two heads are better than one?"

"I can handle it."

Kep glanced back at the flag's stars and stripes.

Visualize Success.

That flag would still be flying when he returned home.

The Revolutionary War (1775-83)

The Revolutionary War was an armed insurrection by patriots in 13 North American colonies against British rule. The war started with the Battles of Lexington and Concord in April 1775. After many difficulties and losses by the Continental army, the patriots achieved a stunning military defeat of the British at the Battle of Saratoga. This American victory convinced France to enter the war on the side of the colonists in 1778. French assistance helped the Continental Army with the final defeat of the British at Yorktown.

Battle of Saratoga: General Arnold wounded in the attack on the Hessian Redoubt

Chapter 2
Strategy Talk

Mule powered through the empty early morning streets and then took the interstate north.

In the backseat, Kep pulled up Mission Notes on his laptop to reread the material on the Second Battle of Saratoga. If Fox could somehow change the outcome of that critical battle, he could change the outcome of the entire war. Kep paid special attention to the players involved in that battle, clicking on the picture of British General John Burgoyne.

Before his team's mission to Boston last summer, he'd barely managed a C- in his American history class. Now he regularly read thick books like *Revolutionary War Battles That Changed The Course Of History* and haunted the library's 900's section, the history section.

Some famous person said, "The more you know about the past, the better prepared you are for the future." Whoever said that didn't even have to worry about a time-traveling crackpot grandfather obsessed with destroying the United States.

Two hours later, they left the interstate and drove along twisting country roads, finally pulling to a stop at locked 10-foot-tall industrial gates. Fencing with barbed wire on top stretched in both directions. Multiple signs warned intruders of thermal imaging and infrared cameras protecting the property.

"You probably didn't expect to be back here and heading off on another mission so soon," Mule said. "I got to hoping Fox got trapped back in 1775 Boston after your last mission. But he's a wily one." Mule glanced back at Kep. "Just so you know, Annie's pretty perturbed about you wanting to travel to 1777 alone."

Kep ignored that last bit and looked around curiously. It was the same facility his team had launched from for their first time-travel trip, but with a lot of increased security. "What's with the military complex look? Where's the welcome to Fort Liberty sign?"

"Closed Fort Liberty down. We've had some issues with snoops."

"What kind of 'snoops'"?

"We don't know yet, but Annie's taking no chances."

Kep's great aunt Annie, his mom's estranged aunt, had founded KRONOS to protect history from time-travelers like Fox. They'd run into problems on their first time-travel trip when a mole named Turner had gotten himself hired by KRONOS. Probably smart to up the security.

They arrived at what looked like a deserted gravel parking lot with weeds and more warnings.

Mule stopped in front of a barn-sized metal shed with giant dented sliding doors. Moments later, the doors smoothly slid open and Mule drove inside. Once the doors closed behind them, another door opened to expose a hidden concrete parking lot with at least 50 cars that must belong to scientists and technicians Annie had hired. How she kept KRONOS a complete secret to the outside world, he didn't know. Did the CIA even know this place existed? She had to be screening employees really close and probably paid them plenty to keep quiet. Or tapped their phones. Or maybe threatened them. Or maybe they were simply dedicated to protecting the country.

Kep followed Mule to a familiar elevator from their first time-travel mission.

As the elevator descended, Kep muttered, "Déjà vu."

The big difference was this time he knew what he was getting into.

The previous summer, Kep and his brother had attended a contest at a Revolutionary War reenactment camp. They'd met their 'teammates,' TJ and Tela, and all believed they were competing for a huge cash prize. But they discovered they were actually being trained to travel into the past, specifically to Boston, 1775, to stop a time-traveler determined to destroy the American Revolution at its birth.

The elevator door slid open.

"Holy—" Kep stared at the subterranean maze of catwalks in yellow and blue and what had to be miles of exposed steel pipes and electronics. It felt like stepping inside an enormous computer. Granted he'd been in the time travel station before, but it wasn't the sort of thing you got used to.

Thick metal cables hung along the walls and the roar of air rushing through giant turbine fans made it hard to hear.

Not for the first time, Kep wondered how Annie had enough money to build this station. How'd she get so rich? Several months after the Boston mission, she'd offered Mom and Dad money. Querishi had arrived at their front door, a check in hand, saying it was "just a little something from Annie to help them through a rough stretch." That they were low on funds wasn't hard to figure out. Dad had lost his job at the university and Mom had gone back to school to get a teaching degree. But his parents had refused the check in a heated exchange on the front stoop that included the terms "bribe" and "blood money".

Kep followed Mule past a gleaming control room with enormous monitors on vast walls. They turned down a narrow corridor and arrived at a conference room.

Inside, Annie waited on one side of a large table.

"Kep." She gave a brisk nod to a chair opposite. Kep stared across at his great aunt and reminded himself he wasn't Annie's pawn.

"Best of luck, kid." With that, Mule left and Kep sat.

A vent over Kep's head blew a steady stream of chilly air but sweat prickled his armpits. Decision time and he wouldn't be bullied into risking the rest of the team.

Across the table, Annie's face twitched with suppressed emotion. Probably irritation that she wasn't going to dictate all the terms this time. Fluorescent lights cast blueish shadows across her deeply wrinkled face. "It's not too late. I can have the rest of the team here within a short time."

"You said Fox was only in the past for 24-hours. He probably didn't have time to change history. It makes no sense to send the entire team on a simple reconnaissance mission."

"I did not ask your opinion."

"You don't *ask* anything. You never did. You tricked the team into traveling to 1775 Boston. And you certainly didn't *ask* if we wanted our genes manipulated."

"We've been through this." Annie's hands jerked. They looked even more gnarled from arthritis than he remembered. "I didn't *choose* to send children. You are all the country has!"

"Your version of the story," Kep said tightly.

"I somewhat regret how I handled Boston. But you're missing the point. Our country is at risk again. You can't take for granted the rights you enjoy as a 21st century American." Her thin lips tightened. "There's work to be done. Debts to be paid."

"Don't lecture me on debts. I was there." Kep had seen firsthand the rebel farmers and grandfathers facing down the greatest war machine in the world at the Battle of Lexington. His own ancestors risked hanging to speak out against the king.

"*I* didn't send Fox back to wreck the country."

"But you hired him. He figured out his theories *working for you!*"

Annie shrugged. "He might have figured it out anyway. And yes, I hired my brother-in-law. He was a brilliant physicist. But his vendetta against the US burned inside him long before that. Fox's so-called stolen inheritance. Kep knew Fox's ancestors had been fabulously wealthy Tories and when the British lost the revolution, they were forced to flee to Canada. The new American government confiscated their estate and all their lands. They went from powerful to penniless. Even generations later, Fox's father barely scraped together enough to live on. He raised his son on tales of the inheritance the Americans had stolen from him."

Kep swallowed hard. He'd rather forget that his great grandfather had raised his grandfather with such a hatred for the country. Heck, technically Kep had lost that fabulous wealth, too. He could have inherited it. But he wasn't trying to destroy the nation.

"Maybe he went off your radar because something happened. Maybe he's gone forever. Made his Big Adios."

Even knowing his grandpa wanted to destroy the county, Kep had a hard time saying straight out, 'Fox may be dead.'

Didn't being related to Fox make Kep more responsible than TJ or Tela? Their grandpas weren't trying to destroy democracy. Their grandpas probably sent birthday cards with twenty-dollar bills tucked inside and called asking what presents they wanted for Christmas presents. Their grandpas weren't busy plotting to demolish the country they all called home.

And while Fox was Max's grandfather too, Grandpa Fox had nearly gotten Max killed during their first mission. That was reason enough to leave Max behind even if his brilliant kid brother might have had some great ideas for this second mission.

"We can't assume Fox is deceased." Annie folded her gnarled hands. "We must plan to stop him and soon."

"Stop how, exactly?" Kep asked uneasily.

"We're not out to kill Fox, if that's what you're asking. If we did, we'd become exactly what we're fighting against. Dictators kill anyone who disagrees with them. Democracy and rights are messier in the short term but stronger in the long term."

"So, then what?"

"Outsmart him or contain him."

Kep felt relief. She wasn't asking him to do away with his own grandpa. "I'll go. The others, especially Max, stay."

"You underestimate your brother," Annie said.

"He's *ten*! He got *shot* on the last mission, remember? If you try and rope my brother in at this point, or the rest of the team, I'll tip off my parents. Unless you have another time-travel team stashed somewhere, you don't have a lot of choices."

Annie's lips tightened further.

The door opened and another familiar face from their first mission rushed in. Querishi looked very pale. She gave Kep the barest of nods, held out a paper to Annie, and bent her head to whisper something. Kep caught a few low words: time trace cover – ten days not 24 hours.

Annie's eyes hardened as she stared at a printout. "How could this information have been missed?"

So Fox had been back in time a lot longer than they thought. Kep guessed Fox had somehow outwitted whatever time trace system they were using. Who knew how much havoc the cagey old guy had wrought. More sweat dripped from under Kep's arms.

"Our timeline just got moved up. You get your wish. You leave immediately for 1777. Alone," said Annie.

Kep nodded, trying to look and feel confident.

Querishi turned to Kep and as if reading his mind, she said, "Fox used some sort of masking system that tricked our time travel monitors. We estimate he may have been in 1777 for ten days. Your preparation time is limited so pay attention." Querishi flipped on the screen in the room and tapped on some keys. A sketch of a camp popped up, with several hundred armed soldiers and a brightly-colored British flag. "Your first objective is to infiltrate General Burgoyne's camp."

Kep let out a low whistle. "Infiltrate? As in sneak past all those guards without getting shot?"

"That's the goal," said Querishi.

Kep's stomach tightened. "Okay then. Let's talk strategy."

Chapter 3

Time Launch

A white-coated technician connected the last of the time transport's complicated straps across Kep's shoulders, chest, and waist—like roller coaster restraints on steroids.

Time travel to the American Revolution might sound G.O.A.T.T. (greatest of all time trips).

Rebels vs. Redcoats.

Military espionage.

History in the flesh.

But Kep knew the truth: War was no G.O.A.T.T. It was guns, battles, and the ever-present risk of death, especially his own.

Kep had traded his sweatshirt and sweatpants for head-to-toe 18th century apparel. Now his pants were breeches, his shirt was homespun, his coat was made of scratchy wool and his boots were heavy leather.

As he looked around, his heart thudded along with the thumping and bumping of valves opening and closing as systems pressurized.

It wasn't just the physical restraints that kept him from darting out of the transport, out of the time-travel center, back to a normal 13-year-old's life. Kep had fought hard to go on this mission solo, and if Annie and her Corps of KRONOS sensed his fast-multiplying doubts, they'd stop things in a second and send the entire team.

The simple truth was America winning the battle of Saratoga had changed the world. It had given the barely-formed democracy a chance to beat the greatest fighting force the world had ever known. Critically, the win at Saratoga had convinced France to ally with the Americans, sending desperately needed cash, soldiers, and its navy. There was a good reason George Washington created a day of thanksgiving to honor the outcome.

Fox knew that fully well. No doubt that's why he'd shown up on Annie's radar right around those critical October days in 1777 before the biggest, most important battle of the last thousand years.

If Fox succeeded, if the rebels LOST the battle, there would likely be no America to return home to.

So Kep pulled on a headset. And just in case his face was as pale as the moon with nerves, he gave the technician an enthusiastic thumbs up to avoid any second-thoughts on the KRONOS end.

The technician tapped his fingers across a screen by the exit, nodded to Kep, and stepped outside the transport.

The door hissed shut. No turning back now.

The pre-launch status check began. Readouts on sensors would determine a go/no go.

Directly in front of Kep, the display console, seven feet long and three feet high, glowed with touch screens, flickering red lights and dials. Meters tracked navigation, reaction control, radar sweep, and words too long to pronounce.

He was under strict orders to touch nothing. Mission controllers would manage the journey remotely.

Unless there was a problem.

Hoping for 0.0 problems.

Three empty seats were bolted to the floor of the transport. The team would be furious that he'd gone without them. But he'd deal with that when he got back.

If he got back.

He'd stashed his swim bag in a storage locker under his seat. He could bend to the side just far enough to open it. He unzipped a side compartment, pulled out the team's picture, and set it on the console.

A voice crackled from his headset. "T-minus three minutes and counting! The clock is running."

"Roger that." To his own ears, Kep's voice sounded sure. At 13, you never know when a random word will rocket to whistle pitch.

"This is a fact-finding mission only!" Annie barked out last-second orders through his headset. "Keep all risks to a minimum! No heroics!"

Was she kidding? 1777 Saratoga was already a minefield. Did she seriously think he was going to *add* risks?

Kep had no illusions that Annie put anyone or anything above protecting the United States. He suspected her "be careful" order was only to save his skin long enough so that he could go back with the entire team if it turned out Fox had done his dirty work.

"Understood," Kep replied. She couldn't see the eye roll.

More crackling sounded in Kep's helmet.

"T-minus ten seconds … nine …"

Kep's chair started vibrating so hard the glowing numbers on the screen in front blurred.

The entire transport shook like it was coming apart, and the team's picture crashed to the floor.

Stupid to leave a loose object on the console. He should have known better. Hopefully, that was his last mistake on the mission.

He braced himself. Time transport was no amusement park ride.

"Eight … seven …"

Kep sucked in a deep breath.

"Four … three … two…"

The transport rocketed forward. The acceleration pushed him harder into his seat.

Going fast.

Ridiculously fast.

Eye-watering fast.

The pressure on his rib cage increased, squeezing him.

Boom!

Shockwaves formed as he punched through time dimensions.

Then...

Silence and stillness.

The journey out of one century and into another had begun.

Battles of Saratoga

Two critical battles of Saratoga occurred eighteen days apart in September and October 1777. The Continental Army's victory was a crucial turning point in the Revolutionary War.

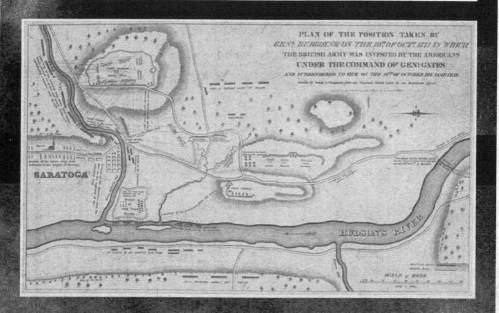

General Burgoyne's position on October 10, 1777

Chapter 4

1777 Arrival

The instrument panel beeped when Kep cautiously unclicked his restraints. Journey by time transport felt like being strapped into a go-cart and sent off a cliff. But with his destination two hundred plus years away, no other travel option was available.

He got to his feet slowly, wanting to finish the mission but also scared to start it. On the team's first mission to Boston 1775, not only had his little brother gotten shot, TJ had been arrested as a runaway slave, and Tela had gotten so sick she'd barely made the return trip. Kep still had nightmares.

He grabbed the framed photo from the floor. The glass had cracked. A bad omen?

At least the empty seats meant his teammates were safe. Max was probably working on some science experiment in the basement, TJ maybe at a casting call, and Tela likely marching at some animal rights protest. Safely living their normal lives. That validated the decision he'd made, no matter how mad they were going to be.

He shoved the photo back into his swim bag in the bolted storage locker under his seat. From the locker, he took a worn canvas haversack, the size of a school backpack, that was stuffed with "historically correct" supplies. He shouldered it, then took a small lantern, the equivalent of an 18th century flashlight, from a second metal locker and stepped toward the exit.

The door opened to reveal a dark and damp-smelling concrete tunnel. The heaviness of the humid air reminded him of a subway station in Chicago. If the station happened to be a time portal to 1777.

From his haversack, he pulled out a tinderbox and using its flint and tinder, lit the lantern's wick. He stepped into the tunnel, and a moment later, the transport door slid shut, leaving him with only the lantern's flame for light.

In movies and books, spies got cool gadgets. Agent Kep got squat. Annie had strict rules about not carrying modern inventions into the past because of the risk of disrupting timelines. He could think of dozens of handy items to use on this trip. Even a basic flashlight would be super helpful if he had to return to this transport site in the dead of night, maybe on the run, but those options were off the table.

Annie had told him he'd find the portal exit approximately 30 feet to the north of the transport. From his haversack, he pulled a compass.

When he came to what appeared to be a solid wall, as he'd been instructed, he pressed a tiny glowing button, like a doorbell. The wall slid open about a foot to reveal a gloomy stone and dirt cave.

Kep crossed into the cave, where the air had a musky, moldy smell. The door behind him rolled shut with a loud thump.

A wave of nerves crackled through him. A war waited outside, and he was headed right into it.

Just take it a step at a time.

That was one of Mom's favorite sayings. He wished he could have said goodbye to her, but it would have been too risky. While part of Dad's brain was always occupied with physics, Mom had this laser-like ability to focus on her sons. He'd swear she could read minds, at least his and Max's, just by looking at their faces. She'd be getting back home from her class soon, well soon as in two hundred plus years from now.

Kep directed the yellow glow of his lantern low to the cave's floor. Snakes, including copperheads and rattlesnakes, hibernated in New York caves, and he didn't want to run into any.

He moved slowly forward and slammed his head.

Ouch!

His fingers touched something slimy and dripping. A stalactite. Head pounding, he continued bent over so he didn't knock into any more. Those things took a thousand years to grow a couple inches. And since he was in 1777 to "save history" he might as well not damage stuff much older.

The light grew as he neared the cave's exit. He extinguished the lantern and belly crawled the last five feet over dirt and small rocks to a hole the size of a doggy door. He squeezed through and found himself in a woodland, cold and damp.

A ghostly, low-lying fog blanketed the area like smoke over a battlefield and sent a shiver crackling down Kep's spine. Navigating his way through unfamiliar territory was tough enough, doing so in a fog made it even harder.

Damp leaves gave off a woodsy smell in the chilly October air. No planes roared overhead, no traffic noise from interstate highways, no train whistles, no sirens.

And no time to waste.

An enormous white pine loomed overhead. That would be his landmark to get back to the cave. He brushed off the dirt on the front of his shirt and pants, covered the cave entrance with branches, and dug a pocket watch from his haversack to check the time. If things were going according to plan, it should be 9 a.m. October 3, 1777. Four days before the famous battle that would be the tipping point of the American Revolution.

The watch face showed nine. Right on time. So there was no need to worry about exploding cannons just yet. He'd be back to the future before the first shots rang out.

And unlike the team's first mission to Boston 1775, he wouldn't be taking Paul Revere's ride, facing down British patrols, or caught in the crossfire of the Battle of Lexington.

This was more like a research project for school: Gather the facts. Report back.

Most likely, the Second Battle of Saratoga was poised to go off as planned. The American victory that had changed the course of the war, changed the course of the world, was probably right on track.

Maybe Fox had even decided he no longer wanted to destroy America. And that's why he'd disappeared from Annie's radar.

Okay, that was stretching things. That option was as likely as Kep switching to the villain role to wreck American independence.

A cold mist covered the ground. As best he could tell in the fog, the portal was in a woods, thick with vines and clumps of brown, dead ferns. The small telescope he'd brought would be useless in the fog, so he pulled out a compass and a small pencil sketch of the area. Annie's original plan, which Kep had nixed, was for Kep and TJ to investigate the British camp while Max and Tela inspected the American camp. Since the opposing armies' camps were only four miles apart, Kep could check out both. It was a one-man scouting mission, plain and simple.

He tucked the sketch back into the haversack and fished out a floppy felt hat that he pulled low over his forehead. With one last glance at his compass, he started toward the British camp. With details from the KRONOS files, he'd concocted a cover story that he was a staunch Loyalist with information that could be helpful to the British. Hopefully that would be enough to get him admitted to the camp.

Unfamiliar territory in the middle of a war held more risks than he cared to think about, but he pushed them out of his mind and continued cautiously forward in the misty fog. Soon he came to a dirt road still leading in the general direction of where the British camp should be. Thick sumac shrubs with red leaves the color of British officers' coats crowded the road's edges. A pair of squirrels chased each other across the dirt, and birds flashed through the trees.

He passed a deserted house, its door nailed shut and weeds choking its garden. The field next to it was charred black, the crops apparently burned.

Moments later, running footsteps pounded from farther up the road. Kep scrambled into shrubbery at the side, crouched down, and peered out.

Through the misty fog, a small girl came racing down the road. Two enormous Great Danes loped on either side of her.

The dogs weren't leashed. Would they smell him as they got close? They looked like they could eat him for a snack.

The girl clutched the skirt of her gray dress as she ran, and her black braids bounced with the impact of each hurried step.

He'd just stay still as a statue until she and her dogs passed.

The girl tripped. She hit the dirt hard. Kep's breath eased when he saw her chest rise and fall, but she didn't get up. He watched anxiously as one dog gently nosed her cheek.

The last thing Kep needed was more complications, but she was a little kid. He couldn't leave her there, but those dogs weren't going to let him near.

Kep cautiously left his leafy hideout, hoping she just had the wind knocked out of her, hoping this would only take two minutes. Hoping the dogs wouldn't eat him.

"Hey! You okay?" he called.

The dogs tensed, ears pricked. One moved to stand between him and the girl. They didn't show their teeth. The size of small ponies, they didn't need to. Kep stayed where he was.

"You okay?" he repeated, staying still to avoid antagonizing the dogs.

The girl, maybe six or seven years old, groaned, twitched, and jerked her head toward him. Her eyes fluttered open, red-rimmed and round with panic. She'd clearly been crying.

Quickly recovering herself, she grabbed hold of the nearest dog and scrambled to her feet. One knee was scraped and bloody from her fall. "The soldiers are gonna kill him! Gonna kill Grandpa! Grandma said run! Get my uncles!"

Kep's stomach clutched.

"Slow down." Kep peered down the road, scanning for trouble. "What's going on?"

"The Redcoats came. They say Papa is a rebel spy. Grandpa won't tell them where Papa is. They're gonna punish Grandpa in Papa's place!"

Kep had an awful vision of some grandpa being shot or hanged.

The girl's voice got higher and faster. "I gotta get to my uncles! You go help Grandpa!" The last word was wailed, but the order was fierce.

When Kep didn't move, the girl pointed in the direction she'd come from. "Go!" She jerked her fist to wipe her brimming eyes and took off in a limping run down the road again, the dogs on either side.

This was *so* not in the plan. The simple reconnaissance plan. No heroics! No extra risks! But he couldn't just do nothing.

Staying close to the road's edge, Kep ran in the direction the girl had pointed. He had no idea how he could help. But he knew if it was his family in trouble, he wouldn't want someone to just walk away.

The truth was that 1777 wasn't a safe time to be a loyalist *or* a rebel.

Chapter 5

Redcoat Menace

The morning sun tried to break through the haze of fog unveiling rocky hills and river bluffs. Soon angry voices could be heard up ahead. Kep slowed his pace as a small farmhouse, in a clearing chopped out of the heavy forest, came into view.

Slipping through what looked like a small apple orchard, Kep crept toward the house, grateful that the fallen leaves were damp and didn't rustle.

He made it to a long row of stacked firewood and peaked over the top to assess the situation.

Behind the farmhouse, in an enormous garden, a lone red-coated soldier ripped stubby carrots from the ground and shoved them into his coat pockets. Cabbage and potatoes were piled by his boots.

To the side of the farmhouse, six skinny horses with fancy saddles pawed the ground where they were tethered to a rail fence. Beyond them, on a low, open porch, stood a white-haired man stooped and frail, leaning heavily on a cane. Beside him stood an elderly woman, her graying black hair tucked into a mop cap, clutching her shawl close. Between the porch and Kep, a half dozen grim-looking Redcoats confronted the family.

"You have one last chance to inform us where the rebel spy that you should be ashamed to call a son is hiding!" The tallest Redcoat, gaunt and hollow-eyed, with plaited hair held back with a shiny black ribbon, stepped forward and grasped the hilt of his sword.

The odds of this standoff weren't looking good for the old man, presumably the girl's grandpa.

Kep peered back down the road. How long would it take her to get help?

"Likely he isn't the only spy living under this roof." The same Redcoat stomped onto the porch. "Do you help your son conspire against the crown? Perhaps the entire Banneker family is a nest of vipers to be destroyed."

Kep's stomach clenched. Surely these were just threats? But the Redcoat looked ready to shish kabob the old man.

The old man, presumably Mr. Banneker, angrily rapped his cane against the floor. "A man can protect his home. We colonists won't permit a king across the ocean to destroy our rights."

An ugly look crossed the redcoat's face. "Do you honestly believe these rebels chanting liberty for all intend to include people like yourself? It is your king's man, Lord Dunmore, who has promised freedom to slaves who join his Majesty's troops."

Mr. Banneker leaned forward pushing his lined face toward the Redcoat. "I bought my freedom. And I didn't free myself from one master to be chained under another," he said with a bitter growl in his voice. "I'll call God my master, but no mere man, regardless of his uniform."

The redcoat yanked his sword from its scabbard. "I could have you hung on the spot for insolence to a king's officer."

"Your soldiers have burned homes, killed civilians, and stolen entire crops leaving those who did the work to starve in the coming winter. My beard is gray, but my brain is sharp enough to see what the 'protection of the crown' brings!"

The redcoat shook his head mockingly. "And you deluded rebels have convinced yourselves you can fight real soldiers."

"I served in the Seven Year's War," wheezed Mr. Banneker. "I am not afraid of a fight." He jerked his head to the elderly woman beside him. "Get my sword, Phoebe!"

The old woman grabbed his arm, shaking her head. "This is not the time."

Kep agreed with the woman and silently urged the old man to ignore the officer baiting him.

"Old bones here is a military man," The redcoat sent a smirk back to his men. "Shall we test his readiness?"

"I am not afraid!" Mr. Banneker straightened his bent shoulders a few inches.

Kep's heart sped up. He expected the redcoat to slice the man down, but instead, the redcoat changed his tone again. "What's to stop this Washington from setting himself up as King of America? Then use his brigades to crush those who still whistle the tune of freedom."

"I believe you mistake the man." Mr. Banneker's knobbed knuckles gripped his cane.

"Quite the prosperous farm you have," the redcoat said darkly. "Once we've educated you in the difference between liberty from lawlessness, we shall take our teaching pay in forage." He turned to his men. "Let's give the old man a sword. Let him go down fighting."

His men snickered delightedly.

Kep needed to do something. But what? He wasn't going to even the odds. He was one unarmed teen. And a teen under orders not to try any heroics.

He spotted an ax flung on the ground near the split wood, but that would hardly hold back a half-dozen soldiers with rifles.

This mess wasn't his fight.

That's what he told himself.

But his feet decided otherwise.

He stepped from the shrubs and strode toward the porch like he wasn't shaking in his boots. Maybe he could distract these soldiers until that girl with the dogs brought her uncles.

"Stay back, boy!" a soldier called curtly.

Sheer terror nearly made his brain shut down. Just enough gray material was functioning to remind him to play this very carefully. His main goal was to get information from the British Army camp by pretending to be a staunch Loyalist. That required him not to tick off this gang of supposed 'allies.'

Kep didn't slow his pace. "Everything okay here?" The line sounded like a recess monitor approaching a playground fight, but he didn't exactly have experience talking to a band of armed soldiers terrorizing a family.

Not surprisingly, Kep's advance didn't cause the soldiers to scuttle away. Instead, the soldier who'd told him to stay back, blocked him with a rifle. "Did you not hear a direct order from your King's men?"

Kep tried a just-a-Colonist-out-for-a-walk wave. "I heard shouting. I'm grateful to see your honors. All of us Loyalists are." *Your honors*? That was laying it on thick.

"A Loyalist? In this den of rebel rot?" The guy who had his hand on the hilt of his sword, the leader, or so Kep assumed because he had the fanciest uniform, swiveled to face him.

"Totally!" Kep needed to stay on the good side of the bad guys. Keep them talking instead of swinging swords until help could arrive. "God save the King!"

"Captain Parr, do you want me to toss him?" the guy blocking Kep called to the fanciest-dressed one.

Kep tensed, but Captain Parr merely said, "You're a local?"

"Sort of." Kep hesitated. The old man would know that was not true. "I mean, I'm not exactly from *here* here. I just heard the shouting. What's going on?"

Captain Parr eyeballed him like an annoying bug. But rather than squash Kep, he puffed out his chest and answered. "A Loyalist reported the Banneker farm as a nest for spies. It must be cleared out as an example to brazen colonists who would dare question the authority of the crown."

Kep suspected the speech was more to justify terrorizing an old man than answering Kep's question.

"If we leave this rebel nest, what precedent does that set for others who harbor enemies of the crown? Proper interrogation prevents the greater evil that menaces society. If this family chooses to protect enemy combatants, chooses to promote further attacks by these scurrilous rebels, the family can stand their punishment. A few broken teeth might be a good start."

Apparently pleased with his 'torture makes us safer' ethics speech, Captain Parr pulled himself taller and scanned his soldiers' faces. "The process to quickly obtain information may be unpleasant. It's like making sausage, you like the result but you don't want to know how it was made."

Kep tried to size him up. War brings out heroes and bullies, that much Kep had learned from his first mission. But surely this Captain Parr wasn't serious? He was just trying to intimidate the old man, wasn't he?

"We told you! Our son is traveling!" The woman, likely Mrs. Banneker, drew her shawl closer. "We don't know where he is!"

"I am sick of the lies and denials!" snapped Parr.

"Maybe he doesn't know," Kep stated the obvious.

"You would presume to speak for a rebel?" when he turned to Kep, Parr's eyes seemed beadier "Mayhap you are one too? *Pretending* to be a Loyal supporter of our King?"

"No!" Kep insisted, his heart beating faster.

"You colonists open your mouths and claim fealty at your convenience. An innkeeper was discovered changing his flag depending on what army marched closer." Parr's face grew red, working toward purple. "It is the cloak and dagger work of spies that allows rebel bullets to kill our men."

"But they're just elderly people!" Kep urged, feeling helpless. He strained his ears, hoping to hear running feet. How far away did neighbors live in this place? He hadn't seen any other houses, but that kid had been running full speed. Kep needed to keep delaying things until help arrived.

Mr. Banneker rapped his cane again. "We have answered your questions. You shall leave!"

"Silence!" Red spots appeared on Captain Parr's sharp cheekbones. He pressed his sword to Mr. Banneker's chest.

Kep instinctively moved closer, stepping onto the porch. "Stop! Everyone! Stop!"

Parr's blazing gaze shifted to Kep. The tendons in his neck bulging. This was a man barely holding himself in check. "We need to strike fear into traitors' hearts, if not bayonets into their stomachs."

This was escalating way too fast. Kep's summer job at McDonalds included training on how to deal with angry customers. Fries cold? Wrong soda? People could go off the deep end.

Stay calm.

Apologize for their inconvenience.

Offer options.

"Sorry." Kep licked his suddenly dry lips. "It's frustrating when someone tells you how to do your job." *Lame!* But Kep plunged on. "Maybe a solution would be—" Kep cast around for an idea. "We go look for the actual guy you suspect is the spy."

Parr jerked his sword to press it to Kep's chest.

The steel point jabbed through his coat. Kep's heart rate bumped to def con levels.

Kep held up both damp palms, the universal 'no threat here' sign.

One of the soldiers took a half step forward. "Sir, no disrespect, sir. But our orders were not to offend the local Loyalists. Because of the supply situation, sir—"

At Parr's glare, the soldier shrank back.

"You worry we would 'offend' those who should be groveling at our feet as officers of the king?" Parr asked the soldier. "We are here at the report and *request* of Loyalists. It is we who are doing the favor!"

Another soldier piped up. "These scurrying Loyalists with their tales of intrigue. That's why we're in this god-forsaken colony. I say they should take care of their own problems!"

A light gleamed in Parr's eye as he turned back to Kep.

"You claim you're a Loyalist. Perhaps you should demonstrate which colors you fly in your heart."

One of the soldiers called, "Let him be the one to teach the spy's old man a lesson!"

Kep caught his breath. This gang of nasties was out of control.

"I don't think our king wants to do battle with an old man. Soldiers fight other soldiers. Show me a rebel soldier," Kep added for good measure, "and I'll be happy to fight!"

"Ha!" spat one of the Redcoats. "You loyalists with your clumsy ways," spat one of the Redcoats. "You shouldn't be serving among our trained soldiers."

"Let 'im prove himself!" shouted a soldier. "Says he's happy to fight."

Parr touched his sword to Kep's chin. Kep jerked back, feeling a trickle of blood dribble down.

"Let's see if you have it in you to fight for the crown," Parr said.

Don't panic.

"Well–um–I mean, I wouldn't be fighting for the king if I'm fighting you, right? So maybe we just—"

"Loyalists are useless to trained soldiers because they have no skills. Prove that you are worthy to join us. It's you or the old parcel of bones."

"I'll fight you!" insisted Mr. Banneker. "Just give a sword. I fought in the Seven Years War." He lifted his chin. "I'm not afraid."

His wife put out her hand. "Hush, John. You are eighty!"

She turned to redcoats, "Leave my family in peace."

"Your family is a nest of spies." Parr jerked his head toward one of his men. "Jones, hand up your sword. These colonists likely couldn't get it out of its scabbard."

The gang of nasties chuckled.

Kep watched uneasily as a sword was passed up to the officer.

He longed to hear the tread of footsteps or horse hooves or, better yet, a couple battalions of Continental army soldiers coming down the road. This was going from bad to worse.

Kep swallowed hard. There was no talking his way out of this. He reminded himself he wasn't totally out of his element. After their first time-travel mission, the team was determined to be well-prepared for any future missions. That preparation included both virtual reality sword-fighting and fencing classes. But unlike practice, he now faced Parr with no chest protector, no fencing helmet, and no saber mask. And Parr's glistening sword was no rubber-tipped fencing foil.

Parr smirked and held out the sword to Kep. "It's you or the old man. My men are not impressed with the Loyalists who have joined our ranks. Let's see if you are any different."

Kep slowly set his haversack on the porch floor and took the sword. He only had to survive long enough for that girl's freaking uncles to finally arrive. Then it would be their problem, and he could clear out.

If he didn't get himself killed first.

GENERALS AT THE BATTLE OF SARATOGA

Major General Horatio Gates was commander of the Northern Army in the Battles of Saratoga. Lieutenant-General John Burgoyne surrendered to Gates on October 17, 1777.

General Gates has been described as "one of the Revolution's most controversial military figures" because of his role in the Conway Cabal, which attempted to remove General George Washington from command of the Continental Army and replace him with General Gates.

MISSION NOTES CORPS OF KRONO

Chapter 6

Sword Fight

Kep's sweaty palms gripped the heavy sword. Fear prickled his skin as he moved it to ready position, with the blade raised.

A watch-this-now smile slid across Captain Parr's face as he flourished his sword. "Let's see what this clumsy colonist can do."

Parr struck out so rapidly, he caught Kep off guard. His sword hit Kep's with such force, it knocked it from Kep's grasp and went spinning to the floor.

Parr placed the tip of his sword at Kep's throat. Kep recoiled. One step. Two. His back soon pressed to the porch wall.

"Ah. Not much fun," Captain Parr pulled back and gestured for Kep to pick up his sword.

Too afraid to speak, Kep grabbed up the weapon.

"See here!"

Some part of Kep's brain registered the old man's voice, but the larger part told him he faced an experienced swordsman. If he had any chance of staying alive, he needed 100 percent focus.

"Shall I split him in two as we do chickens back home?" Parr's gaze slipped to his cackling men.

And that was Parr's mistake.

Kep sliced his sword upward, knocking Parr's to the side.

Parr roared something unintelligible and swung his sword toward Kep. Metal clanked as the swords met in mid-air.

Kep lunged.

Parr parried the thrust.

"Spill some Parr blood if you dare!"

Kep parried in rapid succession. Steel clanged against steel.

Again and again, Kep just managed to dodge Parr's sword.

Sweat dripped into Kep's eyes, but he didn't dare wipe it away.

Parr made a furious charge.

Kep leapt backward, making a narrow escape.

Captain Parr shouted. "Stop jumping! Stand and fight like a swordsman!"

Kep leapt this way and that, dodging and lunging so swiftly that Captain Parr's blade caught only air.

Kep made several wild strokes that were easily knocked away by Parr. His only hope now was to stave Parr off long enough to wear him down.

Parr made a series of fierce, rapid slashes, then gripped his sword and delivered a deathblow.

The force of his blow knocked Kep to the side. He stumbled. And lost hold of his sword.

Parr smirked.

Dread filled Kep as Parr moved in for the kill.

Suddenly Mr. Banneker raised his cane and stood between Kep and Parr, his cane aimed at Parr's head.

"Leave the boy!"

A startled-looking Parr stopped. Fury rose into his eyes.

Hoofbeats pounded into the yard, but Kep didn't dare take his eyes off the captain.

"Captain!" A redcoat called. "Captain, Sir! We have trouble, sir."

A curtain dropped over his face and his lips pressed tight. "I will finish with you later."

Kep didn't know if he meant Mr. Banneker or Kep.

Too tense to breathe and not exactly full of trust, Kep scrambled to his feet and whispered, "Thanks!" to Mr. Banneker.

Mr. Banneker only lowered his cane when the captain shifted to face the arrivals.

A group of ten men and lanky teenage boys rode into the yard. Compared to the soldiers in red-coated uniforms, they were a motley-looking crew with their felt caps and faded coats. But each carried a rifle and more than one had a finger resting on a trigger. The small girl who'd gone running for help now sat astride a horse in front of a powerfully built man.

Mr. Banneker stood as straight as his stooped shoulders would allow and nodded to the newcomers. "My sons and grandsons. I taught all those boys to handle a gun."

The captain, his sword still out but at his side, eyed the group, taking his time.

Kep's hopes rose. The captain had to see he was outnumbered.

"You are to disperse." Captain Parr addressed the newcomers as his soldiers shifted and tightened their grips on their guns. "Under orders of your King's men."

"We watch out for our families," said the powerfully built man in measured tones. "That is my mother on the porch. I don't know how you do things in London, but we protect our womenfolk."

"And we are extra watchful," said a man next to him. "As the barbarians in your employ already have Miss Jane McCree's blood on your hands."

Almost as a group, the men and teens shifted angrily in their saddles. One spat to the side. Another muttered, "Vile! Murdering women!"

Even in the tense situation, Kep ticked off a KHM. Key Historic Moment. The exact details of how Jane McCree died were murky, but the rebel papers had made the sad story of her death famous, claiming it was at the hands of Native Americans under Burgoyne's command. The murder of Jane McCrea had been the battle cry bringing more and more men to join the American cause, to protect their wives and daughters from Burgoyne's menace.

Kep held his breath. This was a powder keg. While the Redcoats were outnumbered, they were trained soldiers and not easy marks. This could be a bloodbath.

"Obstructing the King's troops will not be tolerated. Be careful you don't forget under whose dominion you live," said Parr.

The man made no move to leave, nor did his men. Instead, the heavily-armed newcomers pressed forward until their horses were within feet of the Redcoats.

Kep sensed the gang of nasties was having second thoughts. Several Redcoats shot looks toward their horses. Sensing the agitation, the animals swished their tails and pawed the ground.

The captain tried once again. "We have reports this family, *your* family, is harboring a rebel spy."

"My Pa says there's no freedom under a king!" Juba shouted.

"Hush, Juba!" said Mrs. Banneker.

"You have no evidence," said the man. "Best you be leaving." He shifted his rifle, slowly and purposefully to his other hand.

One of the newcomers gave Kep a hard stare, which made him swallow hard.

"If that is a threat to officers and soldiers of your king, you will pay." Captain Parr's eyes narrowed. "Do you deny you're rebels?"

"We're just nicely saying it's time for you to leave," said the man with a flint stare.

Captain Parr stared for a moment, then jerked his head toward his men.

"Mount up."

Jones grabbed his sword up from the porch floor where it had fallen and the Redcoats slowly moved toward their horses, never once turning their backs on the newcomers. Parr followed, walking stiffly, his face a mask.

The soldier who Kep had seen earlier scavenging in the garden came around the corner of the house, his pockets bulging with carrots and potatoes and a squawking hen under one arm.

He stumbled to a halt and stared at the armed family.

"Let Henny go!" shouted Juba. "You, you *thief*!"

"You heard my niece," the man on the horse said in a deep voice. "She'd prefer you not to pilfer her pet."

This time the man lifted his gun and pointed it directly at the soldier. The soldier looked to Parr, reluctantly let the hen go fluttering off, then scrambled toward his mount.

The gang of nasties looked to be heading off, but Kep's relief for the old man became worry for his own skin. Having announced himself as a Loyalist moments ago, it didn't seem too safe to stick around himself. Even if the old man and his wife explained that he'd stepped in to help, a Loyalist wasn't going to be a big hit with these guys. And sticking around to explain he wasn't *really* a Loyalist, didn't feel too safe either. The group hardly looked like they approved of fish-flopping loyalties any more than Captain Parr.

Add to that, if he stayed behind, he'd wreck his chances to get into the British camp.

Kep snatched up his haversack from the porch floor. "Could I-um-come with you?" he called to Captain Parr.

The captain scowled. "We don't need more mouths to feed. You seem to have a soft spot for enemies of the crown, ask them to feed you."

Nice guy, Captain Parr.

"I have information for Burgoyne." Kep refused to meet the eyes of the rebel neighbors even as he felt ice pick stares drilling into him.

A few murmured threats from the newcomers indicated he really needed to get out of here.

"Important information," Kep urged, his throat growing tighter as he stared at Captain Parr's angry face.

Parr didn't say no, so Kep hurried to catch up with the Redcoats, who kept their eyes on the newcomers and their hands at their weapons as they mounted.

The men and teens watched, silent, fingers on triggers. Kep suspected at this moment, they held him in even lower esteem than the Redcoats.

"You can ride with Jones." Parr jerked his head toward one of his soldiers.

Jones kept his gaze directed at the rebels, but he held down a sweaty hand so Kep could swing up behind him on the horse.

Captain Parr rammed his sword back into its scabbard, then whipped up his horse and led his men, trotting rapidly down the road. "Rebel treachery," he muttered darkly.

Kep had the distinct feeling it wasn't over for this family. Bullies didn't like unfinished bullying. But for now, Kep needed to turn his attention to his fact-finding mission. He had a role in the Revolution, too, even if no one here would believe it.

Chapter 7

Inside Enemy Camp

Still shaken from the events at the farmhouse, Kep paid close attention to their route as he rode with Parr's gang. He'd need to retrace his steps to get back to the time portal once he had the information he needed on what Fox might have done.

Overhead an arrow of geese honked as they traveled over hills glowing in autumn colors. Kep noted their southern direction as another clue to determine his position. Sort of an avian GPS.

Sitting behind Jones, Kep felt the horse's ribs between his knees. Fodder must be low for the British mounts. The odious stench of Jones' unwashed armpits mixed with the stale smell of his uniform, the one he'd probably marched hundreds of miles in. Kep wrinkled his nose against the onslaught.

There seemed to be only one narrow road, so it shouldn't be too hard to retrace. At one point, the road narrowed even more as it passed through a ravine with a tangle of bushes and trees growing up both rocky sides. The last of the morning fog shrouded the area, covering any movement an enemy might be making. Kep's stomach knotted. This steep pass would be a good ambush site if additional rebels were waiting along their route.

The Redcoats were silent, but even without drums beating or flags waving, the clanking bridles, creaking of leather, and the hoofbeats of cantering horses would announce their arrival to anyone within earshot.

Soon they came to a bridge crossing another steep ravine with a fast-moving stream at least 20 feet below. Captain Parr's horse shied. As the captain got his horse under control, Kep nervously glanced along the banks for any shadowy figures.

As if reading Kep's mind, the soldier in front of Kep said in a hushed tone, "We'd best be back before the last of the fog burns off. The rebels have picked off more than one patrol."

"We will not stand in fear of a pack of mongrels!" But Captain Parr spurred his horse forward and moments later, the others flicked their reins and the horses' hooves clattered over the wooden bridge.

Kep exhaled deeply when they left the ravine. By now only the barest remnants of mist hung over the ground.

They passed a field of blackened stubble. The soldier with the carrots stuffed in his pockets stared at it. "Rebels are burning their own crops. Their general wants not a single ear of corn left. They'd have us starve," he added bitterly.

Not long after, they approached an outpost.

Considering he was about to enter enemy headquarters, as a spy, Kep's throat clenched. He worried that the guards would question the captain about him and even more nervous they'd demand to search his haversack. Tucked at the very bottom, hidden under a second flap of canvas, were his maps. It might be tricky to explain them while heading into the British camp claiming to be a local Loyalist.

Acting as a spy already felt like walking around just waiting for a trap to spring. He needed to keep his cool.

Kep cautiously slipped the strap so the bag was hidden behind him.

A sentry stepped forward. "Password?"

Kep's nerves remained tight but knowing the password could be helpful.

"King," said Captain Parr.

Not exactly 007 stuff. But knowing the enemy password might also be good information to bring to General Gates when Kep went to the American camp, though he had no idea how often they changed it.

Almost as if reading Kep's mind, Parr looked sharply at the sentry. "Send for a change of password."

Bummer.

The sentry nodded and stepped aside so they could pass.

He was in! Kep forced his shoulders to relax, trying to look as casual as possible—just your average Loyalist teen entering General Burgoyne's camp.

They reached a small crest. Below, row upon neat row of white tents, there had to be thousands, hunkered down as far as the eye could see. Burgoyne had marched over six thousand men down from Canada. Kep studied this city of soldiers that was the population of some small Wisconsin towns back home. Any scrap of information might be valuable to American General Gates. At this point in time, neither army had the intelligence it wanted about the enemy's precise troop numbers, supplies, or arms. There were no satellites to provide overhead photos and although deserters who switched sides were questioned when they arrived, their information was vague at best.

The ground looked rough, chewed up by soldiers walking, riding, and dragging equipment over it. Rutted paths were full of puddles and dozens of giant stumps stood in every direction, as if some giant had arrived with a chainsaw.

Smoke curled from dozens and dozens of campfires, choking the air. Back home autumn fires meant yards raked clean of leaves, football games, and Halloween. Here they meant an enormous army biding its time, cannons and guns battle ready, preparing to crush the rebellion.

The sounds of drums and bugles grew louder and soon groups of soldiers could be seen drilling at the far edge of the camp. To one side refrigerator-size guys marched. They had mustaches that curled past their chins and braided pigtails hanging down their backs. The soldiers wore tall brass-fronted helmets and turned in exact precision as their commander barked commands in what sounded like German.

Kep attempted to count their number, trying not to be obvious about it. The British had lost a lot of soldiers at the first battle of Saratoga, so the number remaining should be less, but it was hard to tell. He could see hundreds for sure. But five hundred? Eight hundred? The number of men drilling for the upcoming attack would be valuable information.

Captain Parr glanced back and apparently noted where Kep was looking, but rather than accuse him of being nosy, he scowled. "King George's hired mercenaries. Hessian princes grab men out of the fields and sell them off to King George like so many head of sheep."

They looked far more dangerous than any sheep Kep had ever seen.

"The disaster at Bennington is on their heads," continued Parr. "If a proper English officer with proper British soldiers had been sent, we wouldn't have been routed."

Kep's ears perked up. "Bennington?"

Another KHM (and a *biggie)*! The Battle of Bennington was supposed to be an easy raid for supplies, but it had transformed into a key defeat for the British.

If history was still proceeding on schedule, the defeat had occurred a little over a month back, on August 16, 1777. Fox had been on the radar recently, not during the Bennington raid, so it made sense he hadn't changed that part of history. Still, Kep felt better that this smaller battle, that had helped lead to the Saratoga victory, apparently had gone according to history. Both the British loss and the fact it hadn't been Parr's preferred "proper British officer" who'd led the raid matched the history books. No changes there.

The officer who'd led the raid had been Hessian Lieutenant Colonel Friedrich Baum, the now deceased General Baum if history remained unchanged.

"Disaster indeed," said one of Parr's men. "The ones who escaped didn't carry any supplies back, and we're soon to be at half rations."

Kep's brain was buzzing. Another KHM. Half rations were a big deal and led to even more desertions.

They rode further into camp where a second group could be seen marching, apparently trying to imitate the military precision of the Hessians, but failing miserably. Parr gazed toward them and snorted in disgust. "A bunch of untrained Loyalists. No wonder we're in a mess." Parr turned toward Kep. "Why can't you people march?"

Kep ignored the question as hope rose in his chest. History was proceeding right on course. The British were in a bad way. The defeat of the British at Bennington. Check. Low supplies. Check.

Kep glanced around trying to sense the morale of the soldiers, which should be rock bottom. Men weren't smiling, but then again, this wasn't a day at Disneyland.

The wind shifted and a sickening, throat-clogging smell engulfed them. Kep instinctively covered his nose with his sleeve.

Last winter, back home, there had been a dead mouse in the wall. The smell of that tiny rotting corpse had made them light candles and open windows in the dead of January. The nauseating fumes Kep smelled now were nothing he could have imagined.

"That is the smell of a thousand loyal soldiers lying dead in the ground! When your heart bleeds for rebel spy families, remember this," snapped Captain Parr. "We must destroy every rebel and every rebel snitch!"

Rebel snitch Kep brushed a drop of sweat from his temple and stayed silent.

Jones turned to Parr. "Speaking of snitches, that snoopy Irish boy you reported to the commander, sir. I think I saw him lurking about the officers' mounts last night."

"The Irish are lower than serpents," said Parr. "The brat is probably waiting to poison the horses. Keep an eye on him. If he's spying, we'll catch him out and he'll soon be hanging from the nearest limb."

Kep, the spy currently walking beside Parr, glanced at the nearest tree and suppressed a shudder.

"They aren't burying those bodies deep enough," complained the soldier riding to the captain's left. "Some groups are putting twenty to a grave. The wolves smell the blood and are starting to prowl so close you can see their eyes glow in the cookfire at night. One man said he saw a wolf with a man's arm trot by like it was a soup bone. Ought to be shooting the scavengers!"

Kep's skin crawled at the grisly tale.

"The wolves aren't as bad as the two-footed scavengers," said another soldier. "Once the sun went down after the battle, those rebel camp followers were out there stealing all they could from the pockets of our dead. May whatever their thieving fingers took choke them in their sleep!"

The soldier riding to the captain's left nodded. "Last night, I wrote that letter to Bonner's wife. I didn't tell her that the husband she loved was robbed while lying on the battlefield. That the enemy had plundered his watch and shoe buckles. I just told her to keep her mind on what a brave and noble husband she once had."

"We will make them pay," said Jones. "That first battle wasn't the end of things."

According to history, about two weeks earlier, at the First Battle of Saratoga, the Battle of Freeman's farm, the British had "won the field" but lost the battle. The two armies fought a mighty battle, going back and forth. By nightfall, the field was in British hands, but at a huge price in men lost and wounded.

"The next battle we'll come out on top." Kep had to get information, to be Gates' eyes and ears, no matter how horrifying the tales were. "We lost—how many? I heard a lot." He didn't know how to ask this more subtly.

"The rebels fought better than we expected," said one. "Didn't turn and run."

"Don't give those monsters any credit!" steamed Jones. "They are brutes. Aiming at officers! No sense of honor."

From what Kep was hearing, it seemed more and more likely that Fox had not had time to change anything, to finish whatever dirty deeds he'd plotted. Which also meant Kep had been right to come alone to handle this mission. If he could somehow get a final confirmation from General Burgoyne that essentially things were as bad as it seemed for the British, Kep could consider it mission complete from the British end. Burgoyne would soon be surrendering his army, the French would come in on the side of the Americans, and American Independence would happen.

Kep had already told Captain Parr that he had information for General Burgyone. This was the moment to brazen it out and see the big guy himself. "I'd like to see General Burgoyne now."

"Well, he ain't out on parade for your audience," muttered one of Parr's men as if Kep were looking for an autograph, though that *would* be worth something back home.

"I mean to give him the information."

"What is the information?" Captain Parr asked sharply.

Was he suspicious?

The thought set Kep's stomach churning with nervous acid. Working undercover meant thinking one thing while acting and saying the opposite. "My uncle said I could only tell General Burgoyne himself."

GENERALS AT THE BATTLE OF SARATOGA

Major General John Burgoyne commanded the British and German forces during the Campaign of 1777. Burgoyne was also an accomplished playwright who earned the nickname "Gentleman Johnny" for his tendency to throw parties between battles.

His surrender to American forces at the Battle of Saratoga marked a turning point in the Revolutionary War.

MISSION NOTES CORPS OF KRONOS

Chapter 8

Camp Artist

Captain Parr and his men, along with Kep, dismounted and tethered their horses.

Captain Parr stared at Kep. "If you waste Burgoyne's time with nonsense and make me look bad, you'll be very, very sorry."

Kep nodded. He had no intention of seeing Parr again, so that threat didn't scare him. He'd meet with Burgoyne and tell him the news and assess the British leader's mood.

British supplies appeared to be dwindling, the American camp numbers growing daily after the Jane McCree incident, desertions on the rise, the huge losses at Bennington, and losses at the first Battle of Saratoga, it was all proceeding according to history. Burgoyne would be desperate for information.

"I'll escort you to General Burgoyne," said Parr.

Not Kep's top choice, but Parr didn't ask his opinion so he followed the captain away from the rest of the group.

The further into the encampment, the further behind enemy lines, the more difficult his last-minute dash to freedom would be. But this was no time for chickening out. The trickiest part of the mission lay just ahead. Everyone knew how Nathan Hale's spy mission had turned out. Well, Kep hadn't known until recently. History always seemed boring dates and names and it wasn't until he realized every person's life was connected to history and he was tasked with time traveling to save that history, that he began paying attention.

Nathan Hale had been just 21 years old when he was caught with secret documents in his shoe. He'd been hanged by order of General Howe.

Would General Burgoyne hang a 14-year-old boy Kep wondered with a shudder?

The damp smell of the Hudson River crept across the air. Another group drilled in the distance wearing green jackets and round black hats. Canadians, maybe? Kep tried to count their numbers too.

The group continued along the rutted paths deeper into the camp. Near a small stream, women with red-chapped hands washed laundry, and a dozen kids screamed and shouted as they played hide and seek between clothes strung on lines tied between trees. It sounded like a school playground instead of the middle of an army camp.

Further on, women in ragged dresses bustled about, tending pots that hung over campfires. He knew camp followers, mostly the wives of soldiers, traveled with the army. Some were sutlers, like store owners, who sold provisions. Others did laundry, sewing, and nursing. He studied them, hoping for some clue. Did they realize their side was in a giant mess? And what happened to these people when the British surrendered the army? Did they go with Burgoyne's captured army? Or go back home?

"A lot of civilians," commented Kep. Maybe Parr would offer something of value if he could keep him talking.

Parr looked irritated. "More Loyalists arriving by the day, wanting food and shelter. Probably the American camp turned them away, so now they claim to be devoted to the crown."

Two enormous tents sprawled straight ahead. They looked like circus tents compared to the little a-frame regular soldier tents. Clearly, tent size went along with rank.

Kep reminded himself Burgoyne should welcome him. The man had no phone, no email, no text, and no radio to send or receive information. And his messengers had mostly been caught and hung before delivering letters to or from the general. He had to be at his wit's end as Kep's grandpa would say. His other, *normal* grandpa that was. Why couldn't Grandpa Fox be more like Grandpa Westguard, a non-time traveler who loved rather than wanted to destroy America?

Outside the tents, several men looked sleepy as they sprawled under a dead tree with a large cavity halfway up. Further away, a guy, apparently an artist, sat on a stump with a sketchbook, busily drawing with charcoal.

Two red-coated sentries stood in front of the tent, like mastiffs on guard.

Captain Parr stalked toward the sentries and demanded to see Burgoyne.

Kep took a deep breath.

But the sentry shook his head at Captain Parr. "You'll need to see Burgoyne's aide and get an appointment."

"I have critical information." Parr shot a warning look at Kep as if to say this better be critical or your head is my lunch.

Kep nodded vigorously.

"You still need an appointment."

Before Parr's face could turn from red to purple, a thin, extremely fidgety man, like a teenager on energy drinks, scurried toward them. "I am General Burgoyne's new aide-de-camp."

"This boy has information for General Burgoyne," said Parr. "We need to see him immediately."

Kep was less than thrilled with the 'we'. He'd hoped Captain Parr would just drop him off and leave.

"General Burgoyne is quite busy. I will mark down the request. The wait may be a few hours." The aide scuttled away and Parr clenched his fists and paced for a few moments.

One of Parr's men, Jones, approached. "Captain Parr! Captain Briggs wishes to see you."

Captain Parr frowned then said sharply to Kep, "Report back to me when you've spoken with General Burgoyne." And with this, Captain Parr pivoted on his heel and left.

Kep was relieved. The man hadn't given him a place to report to, but since Kep had no intention of ever seeing Captain Parr again, it didn't matter.

Hoping to gather more information while he waited, Kep sank down near two ragged men sitting under the dead tree. The men wore patched red coats stained with black powdered smudges and talked in gloomy tones.

"A man can't live on scraps of salt pork and moldy biscuits," whined one. "Even the horses are living on leaves."

The other man grunted. "My belly is never full. I've heard of men secretly killing the baggage horses for food."

"There's no rum. Not even spruce beer. And with those rebel curs shooting at every man who approaches the river, we're nearly out of water. Last night, Private Phinney's wife, she's a plucky one, went and got two buckets full. No bullet in her head. Don't know if they didn't see her or they spared her because she was a woman."

Another KHM. The Americans were making sure that no foraging party could restock supplies. Check.

One of the men pulled out a carved wooden pipe and clenched it between his teeth but didn't light it. "Did you hear about them waggoneers who tried to desert back to Canada? General Burgoyne sent his Indians after them, then showed those unlucky waggoneers' scalps to the rest of the Canadians and told them the same would be happening to them if they try and sneak away."

The other nodded glumly, then added in a lower voice. "I'd never desert, but I have to wonder what kind of winter quarters we can expect if we can't advance to Albany nor fall back to Ticonderoga."

"At least the frosts will stop the black flies from biting us raw," said the man with the pipe.

"It gets really cold here," Kep, the helpful Loyalist, offered. "We get loads of snow too. Way colder than winters in Britain. Frostbite could be a big problem."

Kep figured if he could help further lower morale in the British camp, he was helping America.

The two men fell silent.

Desertions running rampant in Burgoyne's camp was another KHM check, but the fact he'd soon need to slip out of camp without official permission—deserting?—made him uneasy.

To keep his mind off desertions and subsequent punishments, Kep approached the artist who was sitting farther away from the others, hoping to pump him for more information away from curious or suspicious ears.

When Kep reached the artist, the man peered up from his sketchpad, maybe to see if Kep was worthy of a portrait.

Apparently not.

The man continued drawing.

"Do you know how long the wait to see General Burgoyne will be?" Kep asked.

The artist shrugged.

"So you do sketches of the camp?" Kep glanced at the paper and saw rows of tents. It occurred to Kep that if the guy had pictures of the layout of the British camp, that could be valuable information to the Americans. He had some "historically correct cash" in his haversack. Maybe he could buy a sketch from the guy. "You're really good. Do you sell your stuff?"

The artist's nostrils flared. "I send my work back to England for the papers. Some of my fellow artists are now producing for the enemy. Benjamin Franklin portraits bring a pretty penny painted on teacups in France. For myself, being a loyal subject of our king, I wouldn't sell my soul creating portraits of an American rebel."

Another KHM! Benjamin Franklin was in France at this very moment. The Congress had declared America's independence in July of 1776, but to secure that independence, it needed help from England's powerful enemy, France. Benjamin Franklin was begging the French to send ships and troops and supplies using the argument that the enemy of my enemy is my friend. But Franklin was having zero luck. The French essentially said, "Show us you can win a battle. So far we've only seen bumbling."

Soon, however, the Americans would win the Second Battle of Saratoga and General Burgoyne would surrender his entire army. This would convince the French king to change his mind and send desperately needed troops and cash.

Kep, eager to continue the chat and see if there was more to learn, said, "Those traitors will probably be sticking Ben Franklin's ugly mug on their money before long."

Was that overkill?

But the artist simply said, "That'll never happen. Not even the rebs are that stupid."

Kep reminded himself not to count his chickens. The critical Second Battle of Saratoga wasn't won yet.

The artist, apparently done chatting, went back to his sketching. Kep scanned around for someone else to quiz, but the aide came darting out of one of the big tents and approached.

"General Burgoyne will see you now."

Showtime!

Chapter 9

General John Burgoyne
(a.k.a. Gentleman Johnny)

Burgoyne's aide escorted Kep toward the big tent on the left. Despite the knot in his stomach, Kep reminded himself this meeting was the final step of his mission and gave himself a pep talk. He was about to confirm that Fox hadn't changed anything. That meant Kep had been right to come solo. And he'd done a pretty good job gathering information if he did say so himself. Maybe Annie would realize Kep had some brains, too. Maybe she'd stop being so bossy.

He'd already confirmed most of the KHMs he was supposed to. Bennington had been a disaster. The men were about to be put on half rations. The British had lost a lot of soldiers at the First Battle of Saratoga. Jane McCrea's murder had led to a giant groundswell of support for the Americans.

Kep would toss General Burgoyne a bone with some info on the "enemy" that wouldn't really change anything but would give Kep a chance to check things out at the highest levels, confirm history was on target, and the British mood was appropriately gloom and doom.

He wasn't deluded enough to think General Burgoyne was going to confide in him directly, but anyone who'd ever played sports and ridden the bus home after a big loss knows how to spot the air of defeat.

Two guards stood aside as the aide ushered Kep through the tent flap.

The giant tent was divided into rooms. The front room had two men working at desks, their quill pens scratching quickly across papers, probably transcribing whatever last-minute orders General Burgoyne was coming up with.

Soon they'd be communicating the terms of their surrender.

That thought cheered him up. General Burgoyne would be crying in his Cornflakes by now. Well, Kelloggs had yet to corner the cereal market in 1777, so make that sobbing in his soup, and likely watery soup at that, with the half-ration orders.

Kep squared his shoulders. The key to going right to the top was walking in like he belonged.

Kep followed the aide through another flap door into the inner headquarters of Major General John Burgoyne.

He stopped short.

Not just because the aide would soon be introducing him. But because the mood, the vibe, was ALL wrong.

Ten chatty officers lounged around the large table, laughing.

Cheerful was an understatement.

The mood was...celebratory. Like a post-Superbowl party where your team had crushed the opponent and you're kicking back, savoring the win. He wouldn't be surprised to see some high fives.

WHAT. THE. HECK?

This *should* be less than 72-hours before Burgoyne's Big Fail. The first time in world history that the British Army ever surrendered. And more stunningly, surrendered to a new army in a new nation. Burgoyne *should* soon be returning to London a paroled prisoner of war with a new nickname, "The man who lost America."

Sweat gathered on Kep's forehead as he stared in confusion. Next to him, the aide fidgeted, maybe waiting for a break in the conversation.

No one so much as shot them a glance.

Inside headquarters, candles glittered in silver holders on a white tablecloth, like some fancy London dinner party.

Apparently the low on supplies problem didn't apply to the top brass. Every inch of the table was crammed with platters of food, along with wine goblets, gold-rimmed plates, soup bowls, and glistening silverware.

Did they seriously haul all this stuff from Britain, then drag it down here from Canada hacking their way through miles of dense forests and swamps?

But it wasn't just the fancy stuff, including a white-gloved butler topping off wine goblets that threw Kep. More concerning was that these officers should be beyond glum. Instead, forks clinked on plates as they ate through their banquet with gusto.

Kep studied the men carefully, hoping for a clue.

The guy at the head of the table with a wig of white curls tumbling past his shoulders had to be General Burgoyne himself. Nicknamed Gentleman Johnny, the leader of the North American Army wore a red coat with gold epaulets and rows of gold buttons that glittered in the candlelight. The gold theme continued with a gold-embroidered waistcoat.

In truth, Kep felt some awe at being here with Burgoyne and his officers. Gathered around this table were the biggest kahunas of the British army. Paintings of these men hung in museums around the world.

Kep's notes from KRONOS had included the officers' portraits and he was fairly confident he could put names to faces. Admittedly, most of the officers weren't as perfectly groomed as their gilt framed, oil-painted, versions. A grease smear on a uniform sleeve here. Stubble on a chin there. A couple months on an army campaign through the wilderness takes its toll.

The officer sitting to Burgoyne's right asked to be passed the rattlesnake soup. That had to be General Phillips.

The officer to Burgoyne's left stabbed a piece of charred meat on a platter. "I find bear meat delicious, though my daughters always say *nein* when it is offered to them."

That had to be the Hessian General Von Riedesel, the leader of what Captain Parr had called the "hired mercenaries."

A few officers Kep couldn't place, but each would play a historic role in the war.

Burgoyne raised his wine glass causing lace ruffles to flutter at his wrists and rings to flash on his fingers. The group quieted.

"We, of his majesty's army, have continued to display in every quarter of America, the power, the justice and when properly sought, the mercy of the King." At the end of that little announcement, Burgoyne looked straight at Kep.

Kep gulped, well aware he was in the lion's den with a fake story to share. Here to spy for the rebels.

Keep cool.

"My aide tells me—" Burgoyne began. "What is your name again, young man?"

Lie? Make up a code name? No time to think that through.

"Kep, sir." Kep's voice sounded scratchy. He cleared his throat. "Kep Westguard."

"My aide informs me, young Westguard, that you have found yourself called forth on the duty of your sovereign."

"Um-yes!" Kep had to think fast to keep up with Burgoyne's formal British speak. Duty to your sovereign must mean to do whatever the king says.

"A toast to the health of King George III," said one officer, hoisting his glass so hastily that red wine sloshed on the white tablecloth.

To keep the discussion on track, Kep said, "I have news on the American army."

"Ha!" Burgoyne chuckled. "Farmers with fowling guns who call themselves the American army."

"Hear! Hear!" Wine bottles emptied into more glasses.

"The only information we need is whether there are sufficient trees in these North American forests to adorn each with a dangling rebel!" roared one officer as he struck the table with his fist.

Various death threats to "those insolent, arrogant rebels" followed and Kep tried hard to look the part of "team Britain" by nodding and stretching his lips into a grin.

Burgoyne held up a hand and quiet descended on the party. "I pledged our king that I would put down this unnatural rebellion. And so I shall. The rabble in arms, flushed with temporary success and insolence, will soon be forced back under the fist of England."

Having delivered his lines, Burgoyne sat back, satisfied, and glanced toward Kep. "Your news? You may trust your news with these men. They are the finest officers in all of Britain."

Kep twitched his shoulders. He concocted "news" with last-minute help from the KRONOS team. The information wouldn't give the British any advantage, but hopefully would make them trust him.

"Daniel Morgan's men have arrived at the American camp."

No one looked too interested. One man quietly asked the butler to pass the dish of smoked tongue.

"With his—er—sharpshooters." That *should* worry the group. Those sharpshooters would soon be taking down a lot of British officers.

"Anything else?" asked General Burgoyne.

Kep could sense interest fading. He'd be escorted out any minute. He didn't really have much else. Some gossip maybe?

"Benedict Arnold is at camp too," he chattered nervously. "There's news that Gates and Arnold are squabbling. A power struggle. The camp is divided. Some said Arnold might just quit camp."

This wasn't really headline news. And Arnold wouldn't in fact leave. He would be the hero of the day at the Second Battle of Saratoga and in fact, many would credit him with the American win, but this sort of trouble-in-the-enemy-camp gossip should be welcome.

But the reaction went beyond that. There was a stunned silence in the tent.

"What else have you heard?" General Burgoyne asked sharply. Now all eyes were on him. No one ate. No one drank.

An odd look passed between Burgoyne and the Hessian general that Kep doesn't know how to interpret.

"Ve have heard of this American General," the Hessian said, looking closely at Kep.

Of course you've heard of him, he got Fort Stanwix from you. And you're going to hear a lot more about Arnold since he'll be the hero at the upcoming battle.

"Do you have any more information on this...Arnold fellow?" asked another officer.

"No." Kep was out of gossip and nervous at the weird reaction to Arnold's name.

"You risked much to deliver this news?" asked Von Reidesel in a heavy German accent.

"My very neck, sir," Kep confirmed.

The Hessian looked to his left. "General Phillips, what do you think of this boy's news?"

General Phillips studied Kep as if taking his measure.

Phillips. Kep had studied all Burgoyne's generals. Phillips would surrender along with the others after the battle at Saratoga. But huge irony: He'd be released in a prisoner exchange. And here was a twist. Later in the war, he'd go on to fight WITH, not AGAINST, American General Benedict Arnold. That was because later in the war, the American hero of Saratoga would turn traitor and become a Brigadier General in the

BRITISH army. At least Arnold would save America at the Second Battle of Saratoga before selling out.

Phillips took out a snuff box with a picture of King George III on it and leaned back in his chair. "You are too young for our regiments, but you might be of service to the Royalist Corps."

Kep's heartrate sped up. Was that the same as joining the British Army? If so, that was *not* his plan. He needed to get out of camp before nightfall. Would that now be considered deserting? He tried not to think of those now-dead Canadian wagon drivers.

But he couldn't possibly leave the British camp without finding out why the mood was so good. So he nodded, trying to buy time. "I'd be honored."

Phillips banged a fist on the table. "That loyal men are refugees in the king's own country! A rebel mob recently dragged a Tory from his home, poured buckets of hot tar on his body and likely he'll not survive the burns! Despicable!"

Burgoyne set down his wine glass. "Loyal men shall have their revenge when we strike in battle. And when we march triumphantly into Albany, we shall execute the vengeance of the state against those willful outcasts."

Kep nodded vigorously but was even more confused. And not just at the wording, which was very...theatrical. He vaguely remembered Burgoyne was a playwright back in England, but the sheer confidence of "General Swagger" made no sense. At this point the groundswell of support was actually toward the American army, especially after the Jane McCrea incident.

"We will show them at the next battle," Kep said, hoping to lead the conversation to just *how* they were planning to do that.

Instead, a man Kep didn't recognize hoisted a wine glass, "To General Burgoyne. The very Mars of battle!"

Burgoyne looked pleased with this and hoisted his own glass. "With your able assistance, General Fraser."

General Fraser? Kep looked at the man's round, pock-marked face and felt like a fortune teller who knew too much. The painting of General Fraser that Kep had seen in his study notes had been the famous painting of General Fraser's funeral. General Fraser had died after being shot during the second battle of Saratoga. Legend said by one of Daniel Morgan's men, a sharpshooter named Timothy Murphy. Unless something changed, this was pretty close to the guy's last meal.

"I shall soon embark for England and lay the trophies of this campaign at the feet of our king!" Burgoyne turned to Kep. "Young man, you shall be permitted to make yourself of service to our king. My aide, Mr. Beekman, will accompany you to the Royalist Corps where the captain will assign you those duties."

Meaning he was now effectively a soldier subject to military discipline.

"Oh, I mean thanks but—um." Kep still had a lot of questions, but no one listened. They'd returned to their meal and their wine. The aide clamped a hand on Kep's elbow and spun him around to the exit. Clearly, Kep's audience with the great Burgoyne was over. His best option was to act like an eager beaver to the king's cause while he came up with a new plan to figure out what was going on.

Kep forced himself not to let his shoulders or smile droop. He'd entered Burgoyne's tent planning to confirm nothing had changed, confident he had been right to come alone, confident that history was on track and Fox had done nothing to change the time-stream.

Instead, as he left the tent, he was sure something big *had* changed. But he was clueless what that something was. Or the best way to figure that key information out.

It was like a test question and Kep had gotten a fat, red checkmark: wrong answer.

He tried to ignore the wave of doubt. He needed to plug on. He was all America had at this point.

Who could give him information about why Burgyone and his officers were so cheerful, so hopeful? The aide seemed an obvious candidate, coming and going from Burgoyne's headquarters all day.

A moment later, they were outside again in the cold. Once they were away from the crowd, Kep said in what he hoped was a casual let's-talk-team-strategy tone, "Sounds like the general is planning to smash those rebels soon."

The aide ignored him. Thick smoke from one of hundreds of campfires drifted across their path. His watering eyes gave him just enough warning to dodge a two wheeled cart pulled by a braying donkey, then dodge the steaming pile of manure it had recently deposited.

"I wonder how many days till the big battle starts?" Kep tried again.

Crickets.

New plan. Ditch this guy, circle back and talk to that artist. Or maybe sneak behind Burgoyne's tent and try to listen in? Would they have guards posted at the back?

Before Kep could settle on a plan, a woman wearing a blue dress, fancier than most of the women's clothes he'd seen at camp, stepped out of a small wood cabin just ahead and looked their way.

"*Herr* Beekman," she called.

Beekman gave a short, prim bow. "Baroness Von Riedesel."

Kep's ears perked up. Baroness Von Riedesel? That made her husband General Von Riedesel, one of the big-wigs at Burgoyne's lunch party. General Riedesel definitely knew what was up. Maybe his wife did too.

BARONESS IN THE WILDERNESS

Baroness Von Riedesel crossed the Atlantic with her three young children to follow her husband General Friedrich Riedesel. Riedesel was the commander of the Brunswick (German) troops who made up a considerable portion of Burgoyne's army.

After the British surrender in New York, the baroness became an American prisoner-of-war. She and her husband, along with their three children and almost 6,000 captured British and Hessian soldiers were marched to Boston.

The Baroness left behind a journal of her experiences. The journal revealed that she was critical of the lack of security at camp.

During their stay in New York, the Baroness gave birth to a daughter, who was named America.

MISSION NOTES CORPS OF KRONOS

Chapter 10
Baroness In The Wilderness

B aroness Von Riedesel waved them closer with a gloved hand. "Might I ask for your assistance?" She had red hair piled in curls atop her head and wore a blue silk dress. Next to her stood a wheeled cart with a wooden barrel perched on top.

"How can we assist?" Beekman asked in a high-pitched, thin voice. He briskly walked toward her, with Kep scrambling after, hoping to get more information.

In the modern world, reporters can just shove microphones in people's faces and ask point-blank questions. "What's the current plan?" Being a spy was way more difficult.

Two little girls had followed the woman out of the cabin. They were maybe six and four-years-old, and they raced toward a wooden swing attached to a nearby tree.

"You have perhaps heard of the plight of Captain Plumpfield?" said the baroness to Beekman. "During the battle, a musket ball passed through both his cheeks, shattering his teeth and grazing his tongue."

Kep winced. "Man, that's rough!"

Baroness Von Riedesel's eyebrows raised, and Beekman glowered at him. Kep quickly got the idea he was not considered on a chatting basis with a baroness. But how was he going to get information from her if he wasn't supposed to speak? Or maybe what he said was too slangy. Maybe they were thinking he didn't talk like a normal 1777 person and the last thing a spy wants is to stand out.

But then she nodded. "Indeed. The poor man can hold nothing whatever in his mouth. I have been giving him some of my family's Rhine wine hoping the acidity would cleanse his wounds."

Kep cringed. The poor guy needed a lot more than a glass of wine. Two centuries away from modern medicine wasn't a good place for anyone seriously injured.

"That is most generous of you, Baroness," the officer said. "Especially with our stores running so low."

Her lips tightened. "General Burgoyne appears to have sufficient stores of the champagne he is so fond of. Even as our army suffers from cold and hunger, from his quarters come the nightly sounds of singing and the jingling of glasses. I've taken it upon myself to remind General Burgoyne that our men are starving."

Kep blinked at her point-blank criticism of the leader of the British North American forces, essentially her husband's boss. This was one tough lady.

Beekman's face flushed crimson. Since he was Burgoyne's aide, maybe he felt some of his boss's reflected glory was being tarnished. "Your nerves are understandably stretched," he said.

"I grew up following the Prussian Army with my father," said the baroness briskly. "And most recently, traveling through England along roads made insecure by highwaymen, I was forced to stop at a house standing wholly alone in the woods. We stumbled upon a room full of arms and my faithful Rockwell was certain they belonged to a band of robbers. We managed to make it away by dawn to continue our journey to America, but I tell you this story to assure you, my nerves have stood much, and are still quite intact."

"Apologies. I did not mean to question your courage, Mrs. Riedesel." Beekman's words were clipped, his face remained flushed, and Kep would bet a British pound he wasn't the slightest bit sorry.

"So many of our men lie suffering in the hospital. I have promised this barrel of wine to help as many as possible." She pointed toward the cart.

"We shall be happy to aid you." Beekman gave Kep a slight shove to indicate *we* was not, in fact, plural.

Kep grabbed the handles of the cart. If she left, he'd lose any chance to get more information from her. "Sure, um, Ma'am." How do you address a baroness?"

Again, her eyebrows raised. "You are new to camp?"

"A new recruit,' said Beekman sounding a bit friendlier, perhaps wanting to get back in her good graces. "You will have noticed many of these country people are good royalists."

"I do notice that Burgoyne allows them to walk about the whole camp at their option without any restraint," she said. "I'm sure most are indeed loyal to the crown, but it does seem that if some should be pretending, they could gain intelligence and communicate it to the enemy forces."

Kep's knees went rubbery. This lady was way too smart to mess around with. He thought back to Captain Parr keeping his eye out for some Irish boy he suspected of spying. Kep needed to watch his step and he hurriedly changed the subject. "Could you show me how to get to the hospital?"

"Officer Beekman knows the way," said the Baroness, "but perhaps the girls would like a short walk." She turned. "Gustava, Frederica. *Du Kommst.*"

The girls ran to grab their mother's hands. "Where are we going?" asked the older one. She didn't seem particularly interested in Kep or the officer. That was good. Sometimes kids, even little kids, could be more observant than adults. It meant he wasn't sticking out despite being two centuries out of place.

"We shall accompany Officer Beekman and this young man as far as the sutler's tent," said the baroness. "I need to purchase more ink."

"Papa said I can get a book to write in once I learn all my letters." The older girl informed Kep.

"Mama writes in her book right after she and Papa have dinner," the younger girl added, tugging at her braids. "We must play very quietly while she writes."

Writes in a book every night after she talks to the general? That caught Kep's attention. How much did the general confide? The journal would likely be written in German. His teammate back home, Tela, could have read it, but she wasn't there. But if he could get it to the American camp, General Gates would likely have German-speakers there, maybe even some Hessian deserters.

Kep casually studied the small cabin she had exited. Nothing fancy, maybe twenty-foot square with a chimney. One door. One window. The journal had to be inside somewhere.

"Westguard!" Beekman's sharp tone and pointed look at the wheelbarrow meant chatting was over.

Kep lifted the handles. The thing weighed a ton! He struggled to keep it moving forward.

The baroness looked over at him. "Where do you hail from, young man?"

Kep had this covered. He named a nearby town.

"Ah – a Loyalist stronghold indeed."

"Yes, ma'am. Rebels don't risk showing their faces there." Kep strained to keep the cart moving. It didn't help that the paths were bumpy and hard to manage. Beekman did not offer to lend a hand.

"Rebels," Beekman scoffed. "Undisciplined rabble with the temerity to call themselves soldiers."

"I would beg to disagree," said the baroness. "They may not be properly trained, but they seem like soldiers by nature. They shoot well and their freedom inspires them to stand against our cannons with great courage. That they fight for their fatherland, makes them bold."

Kep was surprised to hear her praise the rebels.

Beekman scowled. "They are British subjects who seem to forget this is not their fatherland!"

"Many have lived in America for generations. Perhaps they feel they are fighting for their home," suggested the baroness.

That also surprised Kep.

Beekman pulled himself tall and said through pinched lips, "A proper British subject fights for his *king*."

Kep glanced at Beekman. *And that's your problem. The Americans no longer consider themselves British subjects.*

This squabbling could be seen as a good sign. Allies were sort of like teammates. And teammates cheer each other on when they're feeling victory bound. It's only when a team is worried about losing that the finger pointing starts, like the baroness throwing shade on General Burgoyne. Using that logic, it would seem things weren't going great, no matter how much cheer there was back at Burgoyne's tent.

"The outcome of that first battle, wow, that was a shocker." Kep stayed as vague as possible.

The oldest little girl stared at him. "You talk funny."

Note to self: watch the slang!

Thankfully, her mom shushed her, in German, probably something about manners, then added, "There was much suffering." The baroness shook her head. "They brought three wounded to where I was, including a young English officer whose family had shown me such courtesy during my sojourn in England. I helped nurse him, 18-years-old, and the only son of his parents."

"Did your friend's son make it? I mean survive?"

The baroness shook her head. "Lying on a little straw we could gather. They wished to take his leg, but he could not bring his mind to it, and mortification set in. Notwithstanding the glory of the day remains on our side, the engagement was a dear bought victory."

The word 'victory' made Kep nervous. Tactically, that first battle might be called a victory. The British army had held the field. But they had lost far more troops than the Americans and the Americans still blocked their way to Albany.

A new worry crossed his mind. Could Burgoyne be so cheerful because the British *didn't* lose the first battle at Saratoga?

They passed a small party of American Indians heading in the opposite direction. They looked strong and fierce and Kep tried to inconspicuously count their numbers.

Beekman seemed to notice Kep's gaze.

"Burgoyne only fights with them as the king has ordered it." He jerked his head dismissively as the braves passed by.

The baroness frowned. "My husband has found them to fight bravely in battle. Many have left camp and General Burgoyne may well regret losing their help."

So her husband *did* confide in her. Getting her journal was looking more important by the minute.

"Joseph Brandt is getting a lot of negative press with the rebels," prompted Kep. Joseph Brandt, a Mohawk, served as a British military officer leading Mohawk and colonial Loyalists known as "Brant's Volunteers" against the rebels. If history was going according to plan, many of that group had left right before the second battle at Saratoga after a run-in with Burgoyne about the Jane McCree incident. Burgoyne had lost an important ally and many skilled scouts. Had that changed?

"I have met Captain Brant," added the baroness. "He converses well and his intellect is highly esteemed. When I dined with him, I found his character very gentle."

Gentle warriors seemed an oxymoron. And if your life was in danger, would you want gentle warriors? But the main question was how many remained with General Burgoyne's forces.

"Gustava! Fredericka!" The girls had wandered down a side path, between rows of tents, making a beeline toward a raccoon wearing a collar and tied to a tree, like a dog.

The baroness called again sharply in German, probably telling them to stay back and not get bit but they ignored her and Kep saw his chance. "I'll get them." He set down the cart and sprinted toward them.

They had stopped just outside the racoon's reach, which was smart as the animal was hissing and struggling to be free.

He grabbed the girls by hand and whispered, "Let's play a game of how slowly we can walk back to your mom."

"I can walk really, really slow!" said the younger one.

"Not as slow as me!" said the older one.

They moved in slow motion and Kep looked toward the baroness and shrugged, then exaggerated his own slow pace, making the girls giggle.

"I bet you walk even slower than your mom writes in her journal," he said quietly.

The little one shook her head. "Mommy writes really fast."

Kep nodded extra, extra slow, which made her laugh. A quick glance toward the baroness assured him she was still arguing with Beekman. "When she's done I bet she puts it away in its special spot really quickly so you can go have dinner."

"She writes *after* dinner," the older one corrected.

"Then she puts it away in the box right by the stove," offered Kep.

"No she doesn't." The older one looked confused. "She puts it in the box by her bed."

Kep didn't even try to suppress a smile.

"Have you come to our house?" she peered at him, still looking confused.

They were nearly back to the baroness, so Kep released her hand long enough to pretend to bop himself on his head. He whispered, "I got mixed up. I was thinking of my *grandma's* journal." The bop made both girls laugh.

When they reached the baroness and Beekman, Kep grabbed the handles of the cart and nodded to them, ever the helpful Loyalist.

Beekman and the baroness didn't appear to notice.

Two red spots burned on Beekman's cheeks. "This war could be won by proper British soldiers," Beekman said, "without allying ourselves with foreigners."

"You question the skills of soldiers other than those of your own country?" The baroness's bright blue eyes sparked with anger. "Perhaps you forget it was my husband who staved off the most brutal of the rebel charges in the last engagement."

Maybe Beekman worried he'd overstepped the boundary that kept him employed, but whatever it was, he shut up.

Before Kep could bring the subject back to some specifics on the number of those "foreign allies" the wind shifted, and a smell enveloped them that could bring an elephant to its knees.

The baroness's younger daughter shouted, "*Es stinkt*" and burst into tears. The baroness pressed a silk handkerchief to her daughter's nose, bade the officer and Kep a quick farewell, and ushered her daughters in another direction.

Kep fought a gag reflex.

This smell seemed to be coming from ahead, from what looked like a recently plowed field. Maybe a garden area, but it seemed late in the year to be planting vegetables.

Beekman sped up his pace, and Kep struggled to keep up as they neared the field. Maybe they buried toilet stuff in there? The field had odd lumpy shapes. As they approached, he realized they were grave-shaped mounds of earth.

The closest had something protruding from it. Something with what looked like toes. A purple, bloated foot.

Kep stopped in his tracks.

The gruesome sight made his heart lurch. His stomach squeezed up into his throat.

Beekman shook his head, a handkerchief over his mouth and nose. "Best to move past as fast as you can. The soil is light and the rains came last night. Many of the bodies were not buried deep enough."

Kep gagged again.

"This is the worst of it," said Beekman. "Beyond those trees, by the hospital, it gets better."

Shaken, Kep pushed the cart forward, held his breath, and kept his eyes averted.

Soon they arrived at a roughly constructed hut with canvas walls. Spine-chilling moans sounded from within.

A harried-looking soldier opened the door to one hut as they approached. "We've been waiting for you. Go right in."

"Officer Beckman!" another soldier called.

Beekman stabbed a finger toward Kep. "Wait here once you've delivered the wine and I'll escort you the rest of the way to the Royalists." Beekman scurried away, muttering something about "Frau General."

"I'll be waiting," Kep called to the retreating aide, and then added under his breath, "Don't count on it."

Kep had no intention of waiting there. The minute he unloaded that wine barrel, he was making his way back to the baroness's cabin. One way or another, he was going to get his hands on that journal.

Chapter 11

Flying Hospital

Kep was antsy to drop off the wine cask and get going. There was no information he would gain here. The clock was ticking. He planned to snag that journal and hoped it would hold the key to why Burgoyne and his generals were so happy.

Possibly, just possibly, they were delusional. Or maybe Burgoyne's confidence was just an act, a show. He was, after all, a playwright.

But that seemed a stretch. The other generals appeared pretty relaxed and happy, too. And they had to know the real score.

The soldier pointed Kep inside. "The matron will tell you where to place the cask."

Kep wasn't sure what a matron was. Maybe some type of nurse. He wheeled the cart awkwardly inside the ugly, dimly-lit, so-called hospital tent.

The smell of vomit and stale urine hung thick in the air. No clean white sheets, no white-coated doctors. A dirt floor and canvas walls blackening at the bottom with mold from the recent rains.

Eight rows of men lay on cots or on the floor on small piles of straw. A blanket had been pulled over the head of a body that lay too still. Kep shuddered and looked away.

Several women moved along narrow paths between the cots. The nearest, in a sweat-stained dress, held a cup to the lips of a patient. The man hunched over, barked a cough, then looked dully at the tent roof.

Still standing by the entrance, Kep called to her. "Excuse me." He wanted to escape this place asap. "Where should I put this?"

The woman looked up. "I'll ask the matron."

Kep gripped the handles of the cart as misery expressed itself all around him in groans and moans. No tinkling of forks on china, no glittering candles, no wine glasses hoisted to toast to the king here.

"Westguard!"

Kep jumped.

"C-Captain Parr!"

Captain Parr, the officer who'd recently terrorized the Banneker family, the officer who'd ordered Kep to report back immediately after speaking to Burgoyne, the officer who Kep had hoped to never see again, sat a few feet away on a low stool beside a cot.

Kep set down the cart as his arms became weak.

"I was just going to find you to report back." Kep took a deep breath. Secret agents need to think one thing and say another and it's easy to get tripped up. "I got assigned to the Royalists."

Parr glared at him, his eyes in black circles. He was sitting at a makeshift desk, a plank balanced on an overturned wooden bucket. On the cot beside him lay a pale, thin boy, maybe ten years old, in a rough homespun shirt.

"I'll speak with you once I finish," Parr said sharply. He picked up a quill pen and turned to the boy. "Go on, Henry," he said more softly. "What shall we write to your mother?"

Next to the cot stood the shattered remains of a drum, with the unmistakable hole of a musket ball torn through. Henry's face was flushed, probably with a fever. As nervous as he was, Kep couldn't help but think this overcrowded makeshift hospital was a death trap. Even if a soldier recovered from his wounds, he'd likely get some infection that 18th century medicine was incapable of curing. Would it really be so wrong to drop some hints about basic sanitation? Save some lives?

Henry shifted as if trying to find a comfortable position. "Captain Parr, don't tell mama about the camp fever. Just that I'm in the hospital. And if I—if I end up buried in the dead pit," he turned his face toward the blanket covered body several rows over, "could you write her again? Tell her I died like a soldier."

Kep felt angry at the generals, at the armies, at war itself. It was bad enough for adults, but to bring kids into it was horrible. And it wasn't just the British, the Americans used drummer boys too.

"You're young," said Parr. "You'll surely recover. Any other message to your mother?" A slight tremble in Captain Parr's hand made the feather quill jiggle as he moved it across the paper. Maybe even bullies have some shred of compassion.

"Tell her Saratoga was a hot battle." Henry's voice got softer. "But I didn't run."

"The hottest battle of the war." Parr nodded, looking weary, then stood. "Rest now. I will see to it myself that this letter is dispatched."

"Thanks, Captain Parr." The boy closed his eyes.

"Maybe they could sanitize his wounds with alcohol? To sterilize them!" Kep couldn't stop himself. He grabbed Captain Parr's arm. "And boil any water he drinks!"

"What tripe are you babbling?" Captain Parr pulled Kep away from the boy. A muscle twitched in his cheek. "Remember the death and misery you see here when you decide to stick up for rebel spies." He spoke in low tones, sheer rage on his face. "Rebels are nothing but armed insurrectionists bent on selfish mutiny. Their anarchy will kill many more if they are not crushed!"

Kep stared, not sure what to say. Captain Parr wasn't interested in germ theory. Parr gripped Kep's arm tighter. "I loathe spies and snitches even more than rebels with guns." Parr spat on the floor.

Did he suspect Kep?

A stout woman with greasy hair pulled tight in a bun bustled toward Kep and Captain Parr. "Put the wine cask over there, young man." She pointed across the tent toward a table piled with folded blankets.

Parr released Kep's arm, stepped to another cot, and bent to speak to the man lying on it.

Kep wheeled the cart down one of the narrow aisles to get away from Parr as quickly as he could. His head was spinning with worries and questions.

A blonde girl with a mop cap and an apron tied over her dress moved toward him through the maze of cots carrying a rope handled bucket in each hand. She stepped aside to let him pass and sloshed water on her skirts.

"Be watchin' yer cart!" She looked up and her eyes met Kep's. She froze, then did a quick u-turn, lugging the pails in the opposite direction.

Kep went into a total brain lock.

No way.

NO WAY!

It was Mary McGee! Mary McGee from Boston 1775. From his last mission.

What THE HECK?

She and her twin brother Finn had risked their lives in Boston to help Kep complete his mission. To complete Paul Revere's famous midnight ride. To help the patriots.

Kep stared after her. She'd given no sign she'd recognized him.

If Mary was here, Finn likely was too. And Kep would bet his life neither had suddenly decided to support the British.

There was only one possible reason the McGee twins were in the British camp. The same reason he was here.

To spy.

"The Irish boy you reported to the commander." That was what one of Parr's men had said about a snitch they threatened to hang.

OMG. That had to be Finn.

Parr suspected Finn. Did he suspect Mary, too? Kep had to warn her!

"Matron." Mary, in her familiar Irish lilt, called to the gray-haired matron. "We'd be running low on water again. I'll go and be checking with the sergeant."

Kep glanced nervously back at Parr, but Parr was intently speaking to a soldier with a bloody bandage wrapped around his head.

Mary glanced toward the tent exit.

Kep's hopes rose. He could follow her out of the tent and warn her that Captain Parr suspected her.

But the Matron shook her head. "Just use what we have. And be quick about it. You're being paid 13 shillings per month!"

Think fast.

How to send a message to Mary right under Parr's nose?

Surely even poorly paid thirteen-shillings-per-month nurses got bathroom breaks. And based on the smell, it was time to empty the chamber pots at a minimum. But some time should elapse before they met so as not to make it too obvious.

In Boston, Mary had helped him by letting him use the submarine she and Finn had built.

They'd called it The Crocodile.

"Water shortages all around, ma'am," Kep said to the matron. "There's not enough water in the entire camp for a crocodile to bathe, Ma'am. Even if he showed up at the nearest latrine at 3 pm."

The matron didn't look amused at Kep's crocodile comment. "Put the cask where I told you, then you'd best be getting to whatever work we're keeping you from. No one has time to dawdle these days."

"Yes, ma'am." Kep shot a glance at Mary to gauge if she got his message, but another nurse had stopped her and was using a ladle to scoop out whatever water remained in Mary's bucket.

Captain Parr lurked at the exit, waiting for Kep, so he couldn't risk talking to Mary directly. There weren't exactly church bells chiming off the hours, but hopefully she could figure out that he meant meet somewhere outside the tent at three.

He had no excuse to wait around. He glanced toward Mary one last time. She moved down an aisle, still holding the buckets. On her left hand, three fingers flashed down and up.

She'd figured it out.

He blew out a breath of relief and followed the captain out the door.

"You gave General Burgoyne your news?" Parr looked at him sharp-eyed.

Kep's nerves were too tight to do more than nod.

"He found it useful?"

Kep nodded again.

"You gave him my name?" said Parr. "That idiot aide might not have."

Freaking out on the inside but trying to look cool on the outside, Kep blinked at Captain Parr. He didn't remember Parr's name coming up, but the man clearly hoped to get brownie points with the British general. "Yes! General Burgoyne said, to um, thank you."

Captain Parr looked pleased.

"Captain Parr!" It was Jones, part of the gang that had been terrorizing the Banneker family. "The men need to know what time we're going back to—" His eyes shot to Kep and he paused for a moment. "What time we're going out on patrol tonight."

"Tell the men it will be a midnight visit." The smile that crept across Parr's face was so spooky Kep half expected the man to sprout fangs. "Not another British soldier shall lose his life without justice being paid."

Icy tentacles wrapped Kep's stomach. The Banneker family! That had to be who they were talking about.

How could he warn them?

Think!

Think!

Think!

He needed to stick around to warn Mary that Captain Parr was watching Finn. Neither Mary nor her brother Finn knew that Kep was a time traveler. They simply believed Kep was a fellow rebel who had helped Paul Revere finish his midnight ride. They also didn't know that Finn McGee was Kep's great-great-great—however many times—grandpa.

And if Finn McGee were here too, spying with Mary, and got caught, that was not only bad. It was a disaster.

The punishment for spies was hanging, and it wasn't only Finn's neck on the line. If Finn got himself caught, Kep wouldn't be born. And if he weren't born, he couldn't travel back through the time stream to stop Fox's plan to undo the revolution.

But before he could even summon any type of plan, Beekman scurried toward him. "Westguard! Kep Westguard! Burgoyne wants you back at his tent. Immediately."

A cold rush of panic. Burgoyne had dismissed him. What could he want?

"What for?" Kep squeaked. He tried to keep his face calm. He didn't think he could keep up this spy façade much longer.

"On the double." Beekman pointed in the direction of Burgoyne's headquarters. Apparently, you don't question orders from the General of the North American campaign.

Kep had an instant desire to dash away. But he was in the middle of the British army camp with thousands of soldiers. The odds of not being caught were zilch.

And he needed to stick around not only to warn Mary that Captain Parr was watching Finn but steal the baroness's journal.

So he put on what he hoped was a glad-to-see-the-great-general again look and trucked off with Beekman to the British headquarters.

This time instead of going to the tent where Burgoyne and his officers had been dining, they went to the other enormous tent. Kep brushed a bead of sweat from his cheek as he and the aide approached the tent that was nearly as big as the dining tent and with the same oval shape. Kep suspected it was General Burgoyne's sleeping quarters.

A small crowd still waited around outside the tents, some played cards, some chatted. The artist sat sketching in the same spot.

"I'll check with Burgoyne," said Beekman. "You wait here."

Kep briefly considered slipping away. But the two guards in front of the tent had heard Beekman's orders.

Kep paced and waited. It was like being sent to the school principal's office. That is if the principal could order you hanged on the spot.

He took a deep breath. There was no reason to panic. Likely General Burgoyne just wanted some more information from a "local." There was no way the general could know about Mary or suspect that Kep intended to steal the baroness's journal.

Kep's shallow breathing made him weak-kneed, so he went over to the grassy area near the artist and plopped to the ground.

The artist was slowly flipping through his sketches. To keep his mind off his nervousness, Kep glanced at them. They were lifelike: Hessians marching in formation. A soldier cleaning his gun. A gaunt, narrow-faced old man writing on parchment paper.

Kep's breath caught in his throat.

He jumped up. "That old man!" Kep jabbed a finger at the sketch. "Who is that?"

The artist scratched his chin. "Don't know his name. He had a bunch of meetings with Burgoyne. So he was handy to sketch. Do you know him?"

"Maybe. He looks—familiar," Kep blathered.

It was Fox. Grandpa Fox. Grandpa Fox who was the very reason he was here. Grandpa Fox who apparently had "a bunch of meetings with Burgoyne."

Burgoyne wasn't wildly optimistic because he was acting or delusional. Something was afoot. Fox had been there. Fox had put a plan underway that gave Burgoyne total confidence that a win was coming soon.

"He met Burgoyne here?" Kep instinctively looked around. "Recently? Today?"

The artist looked startled at Kep's rapid fire questions. "A couple days ago."

Before Kep could catch his breath, Beekman came scurrying toward them. "Burgoyne will see you now."

HESSIANS

Baron Friedrich Adolphus Riedesel commanded all German soldiers in the Saratoga Campaign.

In August 1762, Riedesel was wounded in battle against the French in 1762.He was cared for by the von Massow family and nursed by their daughter Charlotte, who became his wife.

Hessian soldier

MISSION NOTES CORPS OF KRONOS

Chapter 12

Secret Letter

Beekman led Kep through the tent's main entrance into a narrow passageway.

Kep followed tentatively, as if approaching an electric fence around a horse corral and waited for his eyes to adjust to the dim interior.

A second flap led to Burgoyne's inner sanctum. The general sat alone, his back to them, writing at a small desk.

Kep's heart skittered as the aide quietly informed the general of their arrival.

General Burgoyne didn't bother to look up, and Kep didn't know if that was a good or bad sign.

While he waited, Kep scanned the interior for additional exits. Canvas walls hung from the tent roof to create three rooms. This first room, an office, was maybe ten feet by seven feet.

On either side of the general's desk stood two large wooden trunks and to the left of those was a small table with a water pitcher and large bowl.

One of the adjoining rooms that could be seen between the tent flaps held a canopy bed draped with wool curtains. A white chamber pot, like a giant white coffee mug, the closest thing to indoor plumbing in the 18th century sat just underneath.

The opposite side of the tent had what looked like a baggage room. Leather gym bags of some sort and even more wooden trunks.

Unfortunately, despite the large space, the way in appeared the only way out.

At that moment, Burgoyne glanced up from writing and motioned Kep over. "You may go, Mr. Beekman."

The aide nodded and exited.

Kep felt his heart skip a beat.

He approached the general, hoping guilt didn't show on his face. Did Nathan Hale get caught because he looked guilty?

"Young Westguard." General Burgoyne faced him.

Kep anxiously studied the general's face. But Burgoyne didn't look angry or about to throw him in the brig or worse. He looked...glad to see him.

Kep let out a breath.

The general set down a quill pen on a piece of paper and folded his hands. How Kep would love to snatch that paper. Any direct correspondence from Burgoyne would be the best possible answer to the mystery. But that wasn't exactly an option, so he simply said, "Yes, sir."

"By the risks you took upon yourself to deliver the information today, you have demonstrated that your interests align with the glorious cause of the military servants of the crown."

The theatrical talk took Kep's brain a minute to process. Basically, the general was saying he was a good Loyalist. The smart thing would be to play that up. "Yes, sir."

Kep had read about something called mirroring. It made people trust you more. At least according to a YouTube video on spy techniques he'd watched while cramming the night before the mission. So Kep folded his hands the same way Burgoyne had and tried to think of some long words. "We servants must serve his military's glorious wishes."

Burgoyne steepled his hands under his chin. "Your fellow Loyalists have become victims of the dastardly rebels, the hardened enemies of Great Britain. Persecution, arbitrary imprisonment, confiscation of property." Burgoyne's face grew grim. "Shocking enormities unprecedented since the inquisitions of the Roman church."

Kep debated steepling his hands but wondered if that mimicking was too obvious. Burgoyne made the decision moot when he picked up a water glass and took a sip as if to quench his fury. Or maybe he wanted to give his audience of one time to appreciate his dramatic proclamation, about fifty percent of which Kep had followed.

Burgoyne looked him right in the eye. "I suspect you long to find a means to which you might further protect those long-suffering souls whose duty to their sovereign puts them at risk."

Processing.

"Yes, sir," said Kep after what he hoped wasn't too long a pause. "Any way I can help, sir."

Burgoyne looked pleased. "I suspected as much, young Westguard. As you are local, I trust you know the territory?"

"Of course." Kep had the historically accurate maps in his haversack. He should be able to find his way around.

"I am about to present to you a great and noble mission for your king."

Kep had no idea where this was headed but knew there was only one answer. "Whatever I can do to help the noble cause."

"There is a critical letter, that must be delivered to a Loyalist safehouse."

Seriously? Wow! It was like the universe was on his side. All Kep needed to do was detour to the American camp and deliver this letter to General Gates instead of wherever Burgoyne wanted it to go.

"Yes. Of course." Kep held out his hand for the letter but snatched it back in case he looked over eager.

"Admittedly, some peril attends the mission. I feel honor bound to point that out." Burgoyne sat back in his chair and crossed his legs, his brow creased.

Some peril was a massive understatement. At this point in history, Burgoyne had lost many messengers, captured or killed. But whatever American raiding parties were lurking around, Kep was going to give *them* the letter, so he should be safe.

Of course, that wasn't the way to play it in front of General Burgoyne.

So Kep frowned then nodded. Hoping to look worried but committed to the mission.

Imagine if he could hand over to the Americans not only Burgoyne's letter, but also the hopefully crammed-full-of-information journal of the wife of General Von Reidesel! He gave himself a second to relish that vision of success.

"I would be honored to take the letter, sir." Kep met Burgoyne's gaze steadily. "And I understand that there are risks in serving our noble gloriousness."

'You won't be the one carrying the letter," Burgoyne said. "You will be serving as a guide for one of my messengers."

Okay, that was a complication.

The thought of going on a mission with someone like Beekman made Kep's stomach twist.

"Sir, General. Might I...make a suggestion?"

Burgoyne nodded.

"I will take the letter myself. One person is less likely to draw attention from scouting parties than two. I will not fail you."

Burgoyne smiled. "While I heartily approve the steadfastness to our noble cause in one so young, the forests are teaming with rebels and Indians allied with them. The messenger I have selected is familiar with their ways. In this case, two is better than one. The messenger will ensure the letter arrives at its destination. You are just along as a wit—" Burgoyne coughed, then said, "You're along as a guide."

Kep's heart rate picked up a notch. He suspected Burgoyne had almost leaked a key issue, some hidden agenda. It did seem odd, the general suddenly picking a 13-year-old to be a guide.

"Now, young Westguard," Burgoyne leaned forward.

"Yes." Kep hoped for a clue as to what this was really all about.

Burgoyne waved at a wooden trunk with its lid propped open. "Please hand me a wig from that trunk. I think the black one makes me look younger." To Kep's astonishment, the general popped off his white wig, exposing close cropped brown hair, and handed the wig to Kep.

Kep snapped his gaping mouth shut and grabbed the wig, sending white powder puffing in all directions.

Eager to get the conversation back to military missions, Kep hustled to the trunk. Inside stood a wooden mannequin head covered by a black, curly wig. Not sure of wig protocol, Kep snatched up the black one with one hand and plopped the white one onto the wooden head.

He handed the black wig to Burgoyne, who carefully slid it over his scalp and pulled a small hand mirror from a metal box on his desk.

"Better, don't you think?" The general studied his reflection, moving the mirror right and left.

"Yes, sir." Kep wondered if he should say something like 'you'd look great in anything,' but that seemed overkill.

Burgoyne lifted the mirror overhead, and peering upward, plucked at a few strands. "I'll make a note that this one is overdue for delousing."

Even if a response was expected, the whirling storm in Kep's mind had none to offer.

"These portrait sittings. Tiresome." Burgoyne carefully fluffed his new black curls. "But posterity you know. My contacts in London say there's great demand for my image. They would like my most recent paintings to adorn snuff boxes to celebrate our final crushing of the rebels."

The perfect opening to see if the general's plans had changed on account of Fox.

"Do you think we'll be at battle within the next few days, sir?"

Burgoyne turned back toward his desk, mirror in hand, a clear indication Kep was being dismissed.

But Kep needed more information. "Is the destination far, sir? For the letter delivery? Will we be back tonight, sir?" He could hardly add, my parents are expecting me home by midnight from a swim meet in northern Wisconsin, which wasn't even a state yet.

"Report back at 1700 hours for further details," said Burgoyne, not bothering to turn around. He seemed to have noticed a smudge on one of his medals and was busy polishing it. "Good afternoon, young Westguard," he added in case Kep was clueless about his dismissal.

Kep was clueless. Not about the brushoff, but about the general's hidden agenda in choosing him as a guide. Now he had to wait almost two hours. Frustration welled.

Kep tried to focus on the positive. He clearly wasn't suspected as a spy. He'd have easy access out of the camp. And best of all, he had a chance to get his hands on a "critical" letter from the general himself. One that would hopefully give them clues about what Fox had changed.

Still, Kep's stomach knotted as he walked toward the tent exit. He had no idea *how* he was going to get that letter from the messenger, but the future depended on it.

Kep passed the artist who was heading inside with his sketchbook tucked under his arm, apparently for Burgoyne's portrait sitting.

Kep blurted. "Do you know why that old man stopped going to see Burgoyne?"

The artist looked blank.

"The old man in your sketch."

"Ah, yes. I heard he'd broken his leg falling down a ravine. Stupid to be scampering around outside of camp with all those rebel scouts shooting anything that moves." The artist shook his head. "One of the pickets spotted him. He'd strapped a branch to his leg and refused to come back to the camp hospital. Foolish."

"Any idea where he was going?" asked Kep.

"Home?" The artist shrugged and continued toward Burgoyne's quarters.

Fox had probably been heading back to modern medical care. That's why he'd disappeared off Annie's radar. The only question was whether he'd completed his mission before leaving. Whether he'd managed to tip the balance of the most decisive battle of the war in the favor of the British. Hopefully that very information was in Burgoyne's letter.

Chapter 13
Journal Heist

O utside Burgoyne's tent, a quick glance at his pocket watch showed Kep he had less than 30 minutes before he was due to meet Mary and warn her brother he was a spy suspect. The last thing he wanted was to draw attention, so he pulled his cap low, shouldered his haversack, and strolled in the direction of the baroness's house.

Tasks were piling up and jumbling in his head.

Here's what he had to do.

1. Get Burgoyne's letter from that messenger and get it to the Americans.
2. Warn Mary that her brother Finn was suspected of spying and they needed to leave camp ASAP.
3. Steal the baroness's journal and get it to the Americans.
4. Warn the Banneker family that Captain Parr was planning a "midnight visit."

Four separate operations for a team of one. Maybe he shouldn't have insisted on doing this mission alone. If the entire team were here, they could have done a divide and conquer.

Kep desperately wanted to warn the Bannekers about Captain Parr, but he couldn't risk leaving camp and needing to reenter before he met with Burgoyne and the messenger at 1700 hours to discuss the delivery of Burgoyne's letter, which might be the key to this entire battle.

Meanwhile, time was ticking, and he had to make some hard choices about what he could and couldn't do from that list.

Priority one: Burgoyne's letter.

But he couldn't do anything about that until he met back with Burgoyne and he still had half an hour before meeting Mary, so he'd make stealing the baroness's journal the next project.

Kep headed back in the direction of the baroness's cabin. According to his watch, he had less than thirty minutes to carry off the journal heist.

He passed by a small group of women washing clothes in wooden tubs near a blazing campfire. One held a wailing baby. Being a mom without a stroller, bottle, pacifier or disposable diapers had to be tough.

Next, he passed by a group of little kids in tattered clothes and torn shoes carrying bundles of twigs. The kids were trailed by a thin, nervous deer on a leather leash. The deer held potential. If he could get this group to follow him to the baroness's cabin, maybe they would draw the daughters and their mom outside to pet the deer or something. And create enough of a diversion for him to slip inside.

With the vaguest of plans, he approached the group. "Hi. Is that a pet deer?"

They responded with confused looks and a lot of chattering in what sounded like French.

He pointed in the direction of the baroness's cabin. "Want to head this way instead?"

More confused looks and indecipherable chatter.

Kep sighed. "Never mind." He gave a short wave and continued on his way. Two companies of French Canadian militia were part of Burgoyne's Saratoga campaign. These kids might be connected to them. Few people realized how international the Revolutionary War had been.

If his team was here with him, Tela, who spoke multiple languages, could have handed this. But she was back at home, 250 years away, and it was pointless to keep second guessing his decision to come to Saratoga alone.

He slowed when the baroness's cabin came into sight. He wanted to study the setup closer, but one of the baroness's daughters was playing just outside and he didn't want to be noticed. He turned and slipped behind an abandoned wagon to study the layout.

The baroness's younger daughter, Frederika, sat on top of a pile of empty crates at the side of the house, frowning in concentration as she attempted to get a small wooden ball that was tied to a stick to land in a cup at the other end of the stick.

He needed the family gone long enough to slip inside and search.

Through the open doorway, voices could be heard speaking in German. Maybe he could tell the baroness that they needed another barrel of wine at the hospital. But that would only work if she had another one. And even if she did, he'd likely be the one asked to lug it there. Maybe he could say Beckman wanted to see her? But he didn't dare get himself caught in a lie when he was about to be Burgoyne's trusted Loyalist guide.

Any plan would have better odds if he had more than one person to pull it off. But he didn't.

And then, suddenly, he did.

A skinny woman in a mop cap approached the door carrying a covered basket.

Kep watched closely and nearly gave a whoop when the baroness came outside with her older daughter, closed the door behind her, and called, "Frederika!"

Frederika scrambled down from her perch atop the crates. Then, still trying to catch the ball in the tiny cup, she followed the group until they disappeared from view.

Kep silently thanked his unintended ally in her mop cap and looked up and down the wide path that passed in front of the baroness's cabin.

Getting caught inside the home of the German general would be disastrous. He wished the cabin was in a more isolated area, but people moved along the path seemingly intent on everyday chores. A man pushed a wheelbarrow in one direction and several women lugged buckets in the opposite direction.

This might be his only chance, so he needed to make the most of it, and the skinny woman's basket had given him an idea. He slipped toward the stack of crates at the side of the house. He grabbed the top crate and walked purposefully toward the front door.

"Hello! Delivery!" He called out, ready to dash away if a cook or someone responded from inside.

No answer.

The door had a simple latch. A quick glance over his shoulder assured him no one was watching, so Kep slipped the latch and went inside.

The house had only one extremely tidy, bare-looking room. The floor and walls smelled like fresh cut wood. A jar with branches of red leaves, like a bouquet of flowers, decorated a tabletop. On the other side of the room stood a neatly made rope bed, with two small trundle beds next to it.

Gustava had said her mom's journal was kept in a box under a bed.

He set down the empty crate and within three strides he was at the bed. He bent to look underneath.

A wooden box.

Bingo!

He slid the box out, hoping it didn't have a lock. It didn't. He opened the lid and found....

Nothing.

Not even a quill pen.

Frantically, he searched the rest of the tiny house. He found a trunk with clothing, some books in German, two dolls, and a wooden spinner toy. But no journal.

Had she taken it with her? He madly tried to remember if she'd been carrying a purse of some sort when she'd left just now. But he'd been too focused on getting inside the house to search to even consider the option she might take it with her.

Frustration built and built. He needed to shake it off. When he lost a big swim race, he'd trained himself to bounce back by doing two things: recalibrate and take action.

The journal was not here, and it wasn't worth the risk of getting caught by staying longer. He'd have to keep all his efforts now on getting Burgoyne's letter.

He snatched up the empty crate and slipped out of the house.

He placed the crate back where he'd found it and hustled toward the hospital, feeling discouraged. His first big fail.

The Massacre of Jane McCrea

Jane McCrea, a woman engaged to a Loyalist officer, was purportedly killed by Native American warriors serving under the command of John Burgoyne. Her death lead to widespread outrage in the Thirteen Colonies and was used by Patriots as part of their anti–British propaganda campaign.

MISSION NOTES CORPS OF KRONOS

Chapter 14

Espionage Perils

Feeling discouraged, he pressed on toward the hospital to meet with Mary and warn her that Captain Parr suspected Finn of spying.

The good thing was convincing her that she and her twin brother needed to leave camp asap shouldn't be difficult. Only an idiot would stick around with a guy like Parr watching them.

He didn't see Mary in the area around the hospital tent, but there was no clock in there so unless she had a watch, time would be approximate. He'd find a spot nearby and wait.

A rough-looking outhouse sat tucked away behind a stand of red sumac not far from the hospital tent. The smells coming from it made Kep cover his nose with his sleeve.

The worst thing about the outhouse was he needed to use it.

He'd used pit toilets on camping trips and their flies and smells always grossed him out. But a quick peek inside this outhouse made pit toilets look like 5-star luxury bathrooms. There was nothing to sit on, no toilet paper, no hand sanitizer. Just a hole in the ground, nearly overflowing. And the basket that should have held corn cobs, the 18th century version of toilet paper, stood empty. So Kep gathered a handful of leaves from the ground, held his breath, and went inside.

Moments later, back outside and gasping for fresh air, he scouted the best spot for them to talk privately.

Parr hadn't seemed to notice Mary at the hospital and the last thing Kep wanted was to draw attention to her before she and Finn could escape this place.

Kep poked around until he found a small clearing behind dense foliage where they could meet in private. Then he crept back to where he could watch the hospital tent entrance.

The sun continued to arc across the sky, and Kep nervously looked at his pocket watch. Half past three.

Squirrels darted under the trees, rustling through the leaves looking for acorns. A crow's shrill cry sounded from above.

His nerves tightened with every passing minute. But just as he considered the risk of checking in at the hospital tent, Mary came out, looking around cautiously.

Kep slipped out of his hiding place and waved a hand.

She glanced back over her shoulder, then darted in his direction.

"Kep Westguard," she breathed when she reached him. "I thought me eyes were playing tricks upon me." She looked at him closer. "Why you've not grown an inch in two years!"

For Mary two years had passed from when he'd seen her last in 1775 Boston. She must be about sixteen now, and she looked much more grown up, nearly as tall as he was.

Even if spelling out the complications of time-traveling had been an option, which it wasn't, he didn't have time to chat about height differences.

"I don't have time to explain everything." Kep spoke in a low-toned rush. "Captain Parr, that guy I was talking to at the hospital, he suspects an Irish boy of spying. Is Finn here?"

Mary's eyes widened. She nodded.

"One of Parr's men said the 'Irish boy' Parr had told them to watch had been seen sneaking around near the stables. Then I saw you and I was worried that Finn could be the one they're watching."

"T'would be likely," she admitted, looking worried. "Few of us are here. Most Irish hope the devil is preparing a mighty bonfire for the English."

"As his sister, they'll come after you, too! You've got to get out of here."

"They wouldn't be knowing we're related. We gave them different surnames when we arrived. And dyed Finn's hair brown with walnut dye."

Smart move.

"What are you and Finn doing here?" Kep got right to the point.

"I would be wondering the same of you," Mary said. "Surely you've not switched your allegiance to the cursed king."

"Keep your voice down!" Kep hissed, looking right and left. "I'm here gathering information."

"We'd be doing the same," she said in a much lower tone. "Finn's been making himself useful to the officers as a farrier to look after their horses, and I'd be picking up bits and pieces of news from the soldiers at hospital. Getting into camp was easy. They believe most Americans want them here, ready to throw flowers at their army's feet."

"What have you found out?" Kep's hopes rose. Maybe she knew what Burgoyne's big plan was.

"Burgoyne will make a move forward or fall back to Fort Ticonderoga within the next few weeks." She spoke with some pride, in low hushed tones.

Kep wasn't impressed. It was obvious Burgoyne had to attack or retreat soon. He couldn't remain at Saratoga with no supply lines and winter setting in. "With Parr suspicious of Finn, it's too risky to stick around. You've got to leave. Tonight."

She shook her head. "Finn won't be wanting to leave until he's bringing General Gates more information on whether it's a retreat or an attack."

Kep's mouth nearly dropped open. "*General Gates* sent you?"

Kep was shocked the American general would trust two teens to obtain that critical information.

"Ye'd best be quieting yer own tongue!" This time Mary looked around nervously. "'Twas Finn's idea. He enlisted with me uncle's regiment. But he felt sneaking here as a Loyalist to get information would be more a service to the cause. When I found out I threatened to tell our uncle if he didn't take me with."

"He didn't get permission?" Kep stared incredulously. "He's AWOL?"

At her confused look he added, "Absent without leave. They don't even know you're here?"

"We'd be doing important work," she said sharply.

"Captain Parr is *not* someone you want to play around with!" To drive home the point, Kep told her about Parr threatening the Banneker family.

"Captain Parr is the devil himself!" She scowled.

"That's *exactly* why you and Finn need to leave. He wanted to skewer that grandpa with his sword and worst of all, he's planning to return there. Tonight!"

Kep bit his lip, shutting off his own babbling. Loose lips sink ships and all that.

"You'd be warning the poor man this devil is coming?"

"I can't." Kep's gut dropped. "I have to be, um, somewhere else."

"So you'd be needing me to sneak out and get him the warning." Mary nodded, a gleam in her eye.

"No! That's not what I meant!"

"You can't be in two places," Mary said as if it were obvious, then added, "I could be claiming I've a sick aunt outside the lines. One of the soldiers I nursed calls me an angel of mercy." Her cheeks turned pink. "He'd be clay in my hands. I think he's on duty tonight."

Kep blew out an exasperated breath. Then it dawned on him that opportunity was knocking. Time to change tactics. "You're right. You *could* warn him. You and Finn could *both* go! And after you warn him, you can bring whatever information you've gathered so far back to the American camp." And thereby get both the McGee twins out of

Burgoyne's camp and up the odds Finn would survive long enough for Kep to eventually be born.

Mary shook her head. "There's no need for Finn to take the extra risk. You've already said there's danger from that awful Captain Parr. Finn and Pappy are me only family."

You're wrong about that last part. Kep gritted his teeth. "Finn's at risk because he's *here*!"

"He'll not want to be leaving without learning more of Burgoyne's plan. That's what we're here to do. I'll tell him to be extra careful. I can be warning this grandpa about that devil Parr meself.   I'd just need to be knowing where this Banneker's farm is."

Kep felt like blowing a gasket. "Finn *cannot* stay! Getting out of here is *way* more important than whatever scraps of information he might overhear. No offense but remember back in Boston when he went rogue hero and nearly led the British to where Hancock and Adams were hiding?"

Kep hadn't expected to run into the McGee twins on this mission. The fact he was once again having to deal with Finn's insistence on taking on "secret missions" was aggravating.

Mary's face tightened and her Irish accent got stronger. "And *ye've* never been tricked? Ye would be the perfect spy?"

"Tone it down with the s-word!" he hissed, looking back over his shoulder.

For the third time in as many minutes, Kep gritted his teeth. This was lunacy. He was running out of time before he was due back at General Burgoyne's tent to meet the messenger.

He took a deep breath. He had to stay focused. Getting the letter from that messenger was priority number one. Then he'd know whatever plot Burgoyne had hatched for the upcoming battle and get that information to the Americans.

A new possibility occurred to him. "Do they keep tranquilizers at the hospital?" On their first mission to Boston, his brother Max had used crushed sedatives in a homemade dart gun to take down a Redcoat. That might be one way to get the letter from the messenger.

Mary looked confused. "Tranquilizers?"

"Like sleep medicine. Whatever they give these guys when they, um...amputate limbs."

"They'd be given rum at best, a wooden stick to chew at worst." Mary shivered. "What is this tranquilizer?"

"Never mind." Kep rubbed his palms briskly, disappointment turning to a buzz of excitement. Something he hadn't thought of. Something that could solve the issue.

Mary had held off a British watchman at sword point back in 1775, so that they could launch the submarine that had allowed Kep to complete Paul Revere's ride. She had guts and she would do anything for the America that was about to be born.

He was missing his team, worried about dealing with everything, including this messenger, on his own. He'd left TJ, Tela and Max back in the 21st century, but he had the makings of a new team standing right in front of him.

"You and Finn both want to help the cause. And the cause needs *both* of you. This is about more than warning the old man." Kep told her about the letter that the messenger would be carrying to the Loyalist safehouse and Kep's role as guide.

Mary looked stunned.

"Once you're *outside* the camp, Finn could help me get that letter from the messenger," Kep continued. "While you go warn the grandpa guy. Then you two could deliver the letter to the American camp."

Kep was quickly learning the value of backup plans. "And just in case something goes wrong, and Finn and I can't take the guy down, you can tell Mr. Banneker about the messenger. His son is in with the rebels. He could tip them off about Burgoyne's letter and they could be there at the safehouse waiting, hidden somewhere, as a backup."

She still hadn't said anything, but she wasn't arguing either, which Kep took as a sign she was warming to the plan.

"So you'll get Finn to go?" he said.

"I canna be making decisions for me brother," she said. "But I'll be speaking with him. Where would this safehouse be?"

Kep would have to take what he could. "I don't know where the safehouse is yet. I meet with Burgoyne at 1700 hours—"

The sound of footsteps crunching across leaves made Kep and Mary freeze.

Kep didn't breathe until the footsteps faded.

He dropped his voice to the barest whisper. "I'll find a way to let you know where the safehouse is as soon as I meet with General Burgoyne. But I can show you where Mr. Banneker's house is now."

He snatched up a stick, kicked aside some leaves, and drew two lines in the dirt. "Follow the main path out of camp until you come to a fork. Take the road left. It leads through a deep canyon. You'll come to a bridge." He made an X to mark the bridge. "The farmhouse isn't far from there, maybe a quarter mile. It sits back off the road."

"I'd be doing me best to help the cause." She nodded.

And just like that Kep was part of a team.

"The camp's password was king," Kep added. "They've probably changed it by now, but you could say you got it this morning and offering that might help make it look like you have permission to—visit that aunt. I mean if this guy who's got a crush on you isn't there to help you get out."

She nodded again.

"The key is for Finn to get out of camp as soon as possible." Kep drove home the point. "He can wait *outside* the British lines and watch for me and this messenger. I don't have an exact plan yet, but we'll come up with one together when we meet back here. How soon can you get Finn here?"

Mary looked back toward the hospital. "I'll have to be gathering me things first."

"Skip the hospital! Just get Finn and get out of camp!"

"Finn is sharing a tent with other valets, and I'd be sharing one with other nurses. To keep his notes safe from prying eyes, he's got me storing them under the blanket box at the hospital."

Kep flinched to think how close Parr might have come to that blanket box when he'd been visiting the hospital. Finn as a spy was a danger to himself and others.

The thought of Parr at the hospital reminded Kep of the injured drummer boy lying on the cot.

"If you're going back in there, can I ask a favor? For that drummer boy, Henry." He quickly explained as best he could about germs and sanitation, not caring if he broke Annie's rule.

Mary listened intently, but that was no surprise. She was a scientist at heart, having built a submarine in 1775.

"His wound can't get infected," Kep said. "Could you make sure it's clean? Maybe pour alcohol on it? Would you be willing to help him, even though he's British?"

Mary's eyebrows shot up. "As if I'd be catching chill from the ice in me soul. He's but a boy. Of course, I'd be helping him if I could."

"I—er—wasn't sure." Kep felt a bit ashamed for thinking this.

"I've written many a letter for the soldiers dying in hospital. Tis done that I might gather information for General Gates about which battalions have lost the most men, how many artillery soldiers are left and such, but also to let them say goodbye to those they'd be missing so far from home. Once fallen, they're no longer the enemy, only fodder for that tyrant three thousand miles away. Many soldiers here would switch sides given the chance and every soldier leaving tis a great loss to Burgoyne. Finn drops hints to some about how to desert."

Kep stared dumbfounded. "Drops *hints*? Are you kidding? No wonder Parr is suspicious! That's just . . ."

Fire flashed in Mary's eyes and Kep bit his tongue to hold back the word *moronic.*

"Finn convinced nigh twenty Hessians to leave just two days past. What have ye done to help the cause as much?"

"Going rogue hero can do more harm than good!"

Even the dimmest bulb would be suspicious of a supposed Loyalist handing out desertion tips. Kep used his boot to grind out the map he'd drawn in the dirt and give himself a minute to cool down.

"Can you and Finn be back here in thirty minutes?" he asked. "We can't afford any more misses. I already tried but failed to get Baroness Von Riedesel's journal."

As soon as the words popped out, he wished he could shove them back. Secret agents shouldn't be blurting out their plans at every turn.

Her eyes glinted. "That twould be quite the catch! How did ye try getting it?"

"I looked through her house, but no luck."

She nodded, looking thoughtful, then started toward the hospital, saying over her shoulder, "Finn doesn't take to being ordered about. Best be remembering that when trying to convince him to leave camp."

Kep fought the urge to scream as she walked away. He shouldn't have to waste time *convincing* Finn to save his own neck!

He could see why Annie preferred barking out orders.

Chapter 15

One-Man Team

Kep would somehow have to overpower the messenger. Hopefully Burgoyne wasn't sending one of those refrigerator-sized Hessians. And the messenger would have to be tied up long enough for Kep to get away to carry that letter to the American camp. For that, Kep needed a rope.

He passed by a peddler leading an old horse piled with pots and pans, then turned down one of the endless rows of tents. The row looked deserted, probably belonging to one of the regiments out drilling.

The tents were small, six foot wide at most and where they touched the ground, the canvas had darkened with mildew and mold. Through open flaps, he could spot as many as six bedrolls on the bare ground.

He didn't envy the life of a British soldier.

It didn't take long to find what he wanted. Outside one tent, a rope had been strung between two trees. A damp shirt dangled from it, along with a pair of britches and several frayed handkerchiefs.

The crowded tents made a good cover, so Kep snatched the laundry off the line, then grabbed a knife out of his haversack to slice both ends.

He wadded the laundry line into a ball, snagged a couple handkerchiefs from the laundry pile, and shoved the stuff into his haversack.

Rope and gag secured in under three minutes.

He was getting pretty good at this spy stuff if he did say so himself.

He started away, then paused.

Most of the British soldiers here at Saratoga hadn't chosen to come. Often press gangs forced men to join the army. It was a dangerous, low-paid job far from their homes. He reached into his haversack and pulled out a handful of coins, surely more than enough to cover the cost of the handkerchiefs and rope, and left the money on the ground.

Slipping away, Kep felt pretty good. He was making progress.

As he walked back to where he'd meet Mary and Finn, he mentally rehearsed his best arguments for Finn. Hopefully, his great-great-great, however many times, grandfather would see reason quickly.

When he reached the spot he'd met Mary earlier, he slipped into the shrubbery and waited.

And waited.

A bug crawled up his leg.

Someone came and went from the outhouse.

People entered and exited the hospital tent.

But no Mary. And no Finn.

A cold chill raced down his spine.

What if Finn had been caught already! How *stupid* to be telling people to desert while you're working as a spy.

The setting sun cast a glow over the blood-red October foliage in the trees all around.

The tenth check of his pocket watch told him he couldn't wait any longer.

But before he left, he decided to give it one more shot. They might just be delayed. Maybe Finn wasn't locked in the brig somewhere.

Mary now knew where the Banneker's house was, but she and her brother would also need to know the location of the Loyalist safehouse. He could leave them the information, but where could he leave it? He thought of the dead tree near Burgoyne's tent, the one with the big cavity.

From his haversack, he pulled out a leather box that contained paper, a quill, and ink.

Heart beating fast, he scratched out a rough picture of a tent with the letter B. Then a dead tree with a cavity in it near the tent. Finally, he drew am arrow to the cavity in the tree and marked it with a big X.

If he could get the information on where the Loyalist safehouse was, he'd leave a map for her near Burgoyne's tent, in that cavity. Hopefully, Mary could figure that out from the sketch. It was too dangerous to leave specific instructions.

He left the map under some fallen branches with one corner peeking out, right where they'd been standing when they had met earlier.

If she returned, she should see it.

But he had no idea if she'd return, much less if she'd find this map.

He was back to being a one-man team. And suddenly, that felt very dangerous.

Benjamin Franklin

The Americans could not beat the British army alone. The colonists had no navy, and military supplies, such as guns and ammunition, were hard to get. because they depended on Great Britain for most of their supplies. They desperately needed help from a powerful ally.

In 1776, at age 71, Benjamin Franklin set sail for France. His critical task was to gain French support. If his ship had been captured, he could have been executed as a traitor. Instead, he became one of America's first diplomats.

Franklin, one of the best-known Americans in the world due to his scientific work, was something of a rock star in France. His image, wearing a coonskin cap, appeared in paintings, medallions, snuff boxes, and rings.

MISSION NOTES CORPS OF KRONOS

Benjamin Franklin

Chapter 16

Jacques

The evening darkened as Kep hustled back to Burgoyne's headquarters, a feeling of dread in his stomach. He tried to tell himself Mary and Finn had just been running late.

He needed to keep his focus on the letter now. General Burgoyne had called it critical. Whatever plan was underway, that letter was likely key.

How exactly Kep was going to get it was still a mystery. He had the rope and gag ready if he had to overpower the messenger, but maybe some kind of trickery would work.

One thing he wouldn't do was hurt this messenger, even if KRONOS didn't have a strict no-harm rule. For KRONOS, that rule was based on logic. One person's death has the potential to spider-web throughout history and weaken timelines. Because if one person's descendants were suddenly knocked out of the time stream, the threads that hold time together weaken. There was no way to know how many things had to take place for history to take a new trajectory, but Kep's job was to keep as many threads intact as possible.

He soon saw the enormous dining tent that sat near Burgoyne's sleeping quarters. People rushed about carrying trays and bottles, probably setting things up for another fancy dinner. A violinist sat on a stump not far away, tuning his instrument.

It felt a little unreal in the middle of the wilderness. Whether Burgoyne was homesick for fancy parties back in London or trying to keep up the morale of his generals, Kep had no idea. But the general certainly was living large here at Saratoga.

Inside Burgoyne's sleeping quarters, flickering candlelight showed the shadows of two figures, and as he drew closer, Kep could hear sharp tones from what sounded like an argument.

Two guards stood on either side of the tent entrance. Kep gave his name and was nodded inside.

General Burgoyne sat at his desk glaring at a man opposite him. "*You* do not dictate terms to *me*!"

Both men swiveled their grim gazes toward Kep when he entered.

The man sitting in front of Burgoyne had to be the messenger. He had black hair and high cheekbones and sat with his arms crossed, wearing a blue coat, a red wool beanie-type hat, fringed deerskin leggings and moccasins. Clearly not a soldier. Maybe a fur trapper. Wide shoulders, definitely strong.

A panicky feeling rose inside Kep. Unless Finn was somehow able to meet up along the route, Kep couldn't imagine how he'd overpower this guy on his own.

Both men sat stiff and stone-faced.

"Westguard," Burgoyne said. His face looked flushed in the candlelight.

The man in the red cap stared at Kep. "This—*boy*? Absolutely not."

Burgoyne made a sound like a growl. "This is not your decision to make!"

Kep stayed just inside the doorway, worried. There was no way he was getting kicked out of the mission at the last minute.

"I am not under your authority!" said the man. "Your king is not my sovereign."

Burgyone banged a fist on his desk. "His majesty is the one paying your exorbitant fee."

The man turned to Kep and said something rapid fire. Unfortunately, he wasn't speaking English.

Kep blinked.

"Do you speak French?" the man asked sharply.

"Um, no," Kep admitted.

The man turned back to Burgoyne and continued in French. Burgoyne responded in the same language, leaving Kep out of the conversation, which was obviously the point.

If Tela were here, she'd be able to translate. But you didn't need a translator to tell they were furious at each other. Kep picked out the words *acteur* – spoken by the man in the red hat. But if he was trying to tell Burgoyne they weren't just actors in some theater show, good luck with that. Burgoyne clearly loved the dramatic.

The longer Kep was left out of the conversation, the more nervous he got. So at the first break, he jumped in.

"I'm the best guide in all of New York!" Kep lied wildly. "I know every deer path and swamp trail between here and—wherever we're going. And I know where the rebels like to hide out. You probably won't make it without me!" He directed that last sentence to the man in the red hat.

"A boy too young for whiskers," the man scoffed.

"Young Westguard *will* accompany you tonight," said Burgoyne, with an icy look at the man.

The man looked from Burgoyne to Kep and back again. "Taking him will double the price."

"Why you—" Burgoyne flushed even redder. "We had an agreement."

"This boy doubles the risks."

If the guy only knew!

Kep studied him closer. He was younger than Kep had first thought, maybe 19 or 20. Even so, Kep was never going to wrestle that letter from him. A drop of sweat dripped down the side of Kep's forehead and he quickly brushed it away. He desperately needed help with this mission, but neither Mary nor Finn had shown up at the meeting spot.

"Your heritage is showing!" Burgoyne said in a furious tone. "The French have no sense of honor!"

"You may find yourself another courier." Jacques shrugged.

Opportunity knocking!

Kep could hardly spit the words out fast enough. "I can be the courier. I'm really good at this sort of thing! I'd be great! I—"

Burgoyne held up a hand. He appeared to be visibly restraining himself, but simply said, "You will both go. Westguard, you will be guiding Mr.—"

"Jacques will suffice." The man quickly cut off Burgoyne.

Another tense moment followed, but Kep didn't want to lose momentum. "Tell me where the safehouse is so I can start planning the best route." He'd like to ask for a map but Burgoyne was only sending him because Jacques apparently didn't know the area and Burgoyne believed Kep did.

Burgoyne cleared his throat. "The house is not far from the banks of the Hudson, where it bends near a creek. I am told it belongs to a William Bacon." He looked toward Kep expectantly.

"Mr. Bacon, right. I know his house well." Kep, of course, had no clue who Bacon was, but the river bank wouldn't be hard to follow. And more importantly if he could get that name, William Bacon, to Mary and she could get it to the rebels, surely they would know where this safehouse was. And Kep needed their help.

"It will be too dangerous to travel the main roads," Kep said, frowning, "Luckily, I know a lot of backways to travel."

Burgoyne stood and put a hand on Kep's shoulder. "I appreciate that you act for a sense of duty and loyalty and not for sheer pecuniary purposes."

Kep was pretty sure "pecuniary" meant that he wasn't asking for money. "It's payment enough to assist the sovereign. When do we leave?"

"You shall depart immediately," said Burgoyne.

Uh oh. He needed enough time away from Jacques to leave a note for Mary giving her the information that the Loyalist safehouse belonged to some guy named William Bacon and was along the banks of the river. He had to hope she'd gotten his first note, telling her that if he learned the location of the safehouse from Burgoyne, he'd leave a second note in the tree cavity near Burgoyne's tent.

If she could get that information to the Bannekers, after warning them about Captain Parr, they might be able to help out. Juba's dad was supposed to be part of a rebel network. Maybe that network could intercept the letter at the safehouse.

At the bare minimum, if Mary and Finn could find out where it was for themselves, maybe they could come to the safehouse and somehow help Kep get the letter, though that seemed one in a million odds.

"I would like to—um—use the latrine." Kep edged toward the door. "So if you'll excuse me. You guys finish up, and I'll be right back."

Jacques said something to Burgoyne in French and Kep slipped out. He told the guard, "I need to use the latrine. Fast."

"They dug a new slop pit beyond those trees," replied one, pointing. "Your nose will lead you."

Kep jogged off in that direction. But as soon as he was out of sight, he opened his haversack and snatched out a small leather box that held paper, quill and ink. Hand nearly trembling with haste, he unstopped the ink, dipped the quill, and wrote: Safehouse is William Bacon's house. Along the river where it bends, near a creek.

He nervously wafted the paper to dry then folded it.

Two minutes down. Hopefully those guards weren't timing his return from the latrine.

He yanked out the map out of his haversack to study the river, looking for a bend near a creek. The portal hadn't been too far from the river, so he quickly got his bearings, then he paced to the dead tree near Burgoyne's tent, looked around to make sure no one was watching, tucked the note into the hole, and raced back.

The odds of success on this mission were feeling minuscule.

Back at Burgoyne's headquarters, Jacques was now standing, and if he looked powerful sitting down, double that standing up. The guy was easily over six foot. Kep's earlier vow not to hurt the messenger was unnecessary. The reverse seemed the bigger risk.

"You've got the letter?" That popped out a little too eagerly.

Jacques ignored him.

Burgoyne once again laid a hand on Kep's shoulder. "You will report back once the mission is complete, young Westguard."

"Jacques isn't coming back?" Kep quickly tried to figure out how that might work with getting the letter.

Burgoyne coughed. "I meant both of you, of course."

Jacque slung a pouch across his chest and strode out of the tent.

Kep scrambled after, his stomach knotted into a pretzel. This was the most poorly planned mission in the history of spying. Had he actually accused Finn of being a pathetic spy? Kep had one pitiful rope and gag to take down a guy who was big enough to play in the NFL. Things were not looking up.

Chapter 17

Dangerous Journey

A bright moon hung overhead as Kep and Jacques left Burgoyne's headquarters. Kep slid his gaze toward the small pouch Jacques wore. He figured the letter was in the pouch or concealed in his coat pocket.

They passed a small group of Indians, likely Iroquois, a tribe that had sided with the British, and Jacques stopped and spoke with them. Kep wished he could understand. The Iroquois had provided Burgoyne with a key advantage as scouts, but if history were proceeding on target, most had left after the Jane McCrea incident.

Their mood looked grim, and Jacques frowned as they departed, but that told Kep little.

Soon Kep and Jacques proceeded toward the outer edges of the camp and Jacques showed the pickets at the guard station a pass from Burgoyne and gave them the password, which Kep was relieved had remained the same. That meant the one he'd given to Mary was still correct if she and Finn were to get out of camp, though hope on that front was fading fast.

Jacques moved soundlessly, like he was wearing velvet shoes, and when they cleared the British lines and were alone, Jacques made a motion for Kep to go ahead and said snidely, "The best guide in New York shall lead."

"We'll follow this side road for a while," Kep whispered. The side road was the one that led to the Banneker's farm, which meant it was also in the direction of the river. He had no idea how familiar with the area

Jacques was, but the messenger shouldn't be suspicious as long as they were generally going in the right direction.

Compared to the busy camp with its campfires, the woods were quiet and eerie. Kep could feel his skin prickle.

A sudden noise made him jump. A quail fluttered up from the brush.

Chill out! You'll hardly convince Jacques you're some expert guide if a quail makes you jump ten feet.

Kep glanced back at Jacques. There was no way he could wrestle this guy to the ground alone and take the letter. But what other option did he have?

History told him rebel scouting parties patrolled the area.

What if he purposely drew their attention?

If he and Jacques got captured, Kep could tell the rebels about the letter, and they could get it from the messenger.

The obvious risk was that the rebels might shoot first and ask questions later. In an attack, there'd be a risk of going down to "friendly fire," but he could think of no other way to get the letter to the Americans.

Kep's jaw tightened as he considered how to execute the plan.

First, he needed to make sure they were far enough from the British lines that British soldiers wouldn't be drawn into the fray.

He walked along the road quickly until he judged they'd traveled at least a half a mile.

Then Kep shifted toward the edge of the road, where some twigs lay. Kep shuffled across, snapping several.

"You are making too much noise!" Jacques whispered harshly.

"It's these boots." Kep held up one of his feet. "I wish I had moccasins like yours."

"Lift your feet," Jacques snapped.

Plotting his next move, Kep walked more quietly, though not as softly as Jacques, who moved like a cat in the dark.

The woods seemed huge. What were the odds any scouting party would happen across them even if he were shouting as loud as he could?

"This is the turn off." Kep moved purposely into the dense underbrush, snapping branches with his shoulders. "Oops. Sorry! Wrong way."

A strong hand grasped his shoulder. "I thought you knew every pathway?" Jacques's voice was low and furious.

"I—er—usually travel in the daytime. I got confused." Kep didn't lower his voice.

The sharp bark of a crow's "Caw! Caw!" came in the distance.

With jangled nerves, Kep proceeded back along the road until he thought a safe enough amount of time had passed, then crashed once again into the underbrush.

"Oops," he said. "The path's a little farther up. Sorry."

Not sorry.

Jacques stared at him in the moonlight, one hand on the hunting knife on his belt. "If you make any more racket, you won't live to arrive at the location."

"Burgoyne said you wouldn't get paid unless we both completed the mission," offered Kep, much more boldly than he felt.

"For Burgoyne, scalps often suffice." Jacques's face was an unreadable mask.

"I—don't think that's what he meant." Kep walked more quietly. His hands felt trembly and he shoved them in his pockets. He needed to be more careful. Jacques was already suspicious.

They continued on with only the sounds of the forest. An owl hooted once, then twice.

From somewhere nearby, a nighthawk sounded its nasal *pee-yah, pee-yah.*

Jacques reached out and pulled Kep to a stop. He looked around intently.

"What?" Kep whispered nervously.

Jacques put a finger to his lips.

The nighthawk's call sounded a second time.

"That's a signal," Jacques said in a voice just above a breath. He slipped off the road and ran, making his own path through the woods as easily as if it were a road. Kep followed him, cursing his heavy boots. Only his swim training allowed him to keep up.

He couldn't lose sight of Jacques or he'd never get that letter. Jacques might be lying about the signal stuff. Maybe he planned to lose Kep and deliver the letter on his own. Tell Burgoyne Kep was too slow to keep up.

Kep put on an extra spurt of speed.

A moment later an arrow spiraled past Kep's head and sliced into a tree above him.

Jacques sprinted like a cougar through the woods. Sheer terror inspired Kep to keep pace, running at speeds he'd never known he could reach.

A second arrow whizzed past his ear, so close it moved the air around him.

Kep *had* succeeded in drawing attention.

Would he live long enough to regret it?

French Support

The enemy of my enemy is my friend. France, still angry from its defeat in the Seven Year's War, saw America's rebellion as an opportunity for revenge. They wanted to weaken the British Empire by helping deprive it of its North American colonies.

However, France wasn't going to throw away its money and manpower on a lost cause. Many had reservations about the strength of colonial forces, many of which lacked weaponry, artillery, gunpowder, even proper footwear.

The turning point of the Revolutionary War was the American victory at The Battle of Saratoga in October 1777. The success at Saratoga convinced the French to enter the war as an American ally.

Between 1778 and 1782, the French provided ammunition, arms, uniforms, supplies, and, most importantly, troops and naval support to the Continental Army.

French King
Louis XVI

MISSION NOTES CORPS OF KRONOS

Chapter 18

Pact

Kep sprinted through the woods. His heart slammed against his ribcage and he pumped his legs even faster.

Just ahead, Jacques veered to the left.

Kep followed, stumbling over thick tree roots. They reached the edge of a ravine and scrambled down, dirt and rocks scattering.

He started sliding and grabbed a branch to steady himself.

Just below him, Jacques went statue still.

Kep did the same, panting in breaths, holding onto the branch that was keeping him from sliding down the steep bank to the shadowy rocks and prickly underbrush below him.

Rustling that could have been human or animal sounded nearby.

Cold fear spread through his veins. Kep's fingers stretched to cracking and his arms shook from the strain, but he didn't so much as twitch a muscle. He thought of his parents. Of Max. Of Grandpa Westguard and TJ and Tela. Would he ever see them again?

The sounds eventually faded. In the moonlight, he could see Jacques shake his head.

Don't move yet.

Kep pushed the toe of his boot into the dirt of the bank, to lessen the strain on his shoulders.

Finally, Jacques glanced up at him and pointed to a rock outcropping further down the steep hill.

Kep nodded.

They moved toward the outcropping. Kep moved as noiselessly as possible, half climbing, half sliding down the steep bank. When he lost his footing, kicking loose gravel that went scratching downward, Jacques sent a bitter scowl his way.

The rock outcropping had a small cave underneath. Jacques bent to enter and Kep followed.

Jacques whispered, "We'll stay until we're sure they've moved on."

They sat, hunched over, in the tiny cave, in a shaft of moonlight.

Kep forced his breathing to slow down.

His attempt to attract a scouting party had backfired. He'd attracted them all right and he was lucky to still be in the land of the living.

Still, history showed that the right message delivered at the right time could change the course of the war. Paul Revere's midnight ride had proven that.

And that letter Jacques carried from General Burgoyne could mean the difference between victory and defeat for the Americans.

Kep's gaze slid to the knife at Jacques belt. A polished wood handle stuck from a stitched leather sheath. The steel blade inside that sheath could easily end up plunged into his chest if he made the wrong move.

He couldn't hold out hope for Finn and Mary somehow coming to help. Mary probably hadn't found his note. Kep was on his own.

To be less than five feet from what might be the most critical letter of the revolution but unable to get it was driving him crazy. He'd give a million bucks to be able to snag it.

A million bucks.

That's when the idea hit him.

Kep's haversack lay next to him, in a sliver of moonlight. Very quietly, he reached into it for the cloth pouch that served as an 18th century wallet.

From the corner of his eye, he could see Jacques was watching him.

Messengers weren't soldiers. Jacques himself said the king wasn't his sovereign. This guy wasn't some Loyalist diehard. Burgyone was furious that Jacque had doubled the charge for the mission. Clearly, money was his basic motive. Maybe he would hand over the letter for more of it.

Kep pulled out a fistful of coins and stacked them on the dirt floor of the cave. He reached for another handful.

This could be a stupid move. Jacques could try and take the money by force and still deliver the letter. But delivering the letter clearly had its own dangers. Jacques might well be happy to turn it over.

Kep had a lot of "period appropriate" coins with him. Annie had either bought up boatloads of antique money off eBay or maybe she had someone counterfeiting them, but either way, Kep wasn't certain of the denominations and cursed himself for not asking exactly how much he'd been sent with. Something like copper farthings and silver half crowns. Then there were shillings and guineas, but his nervous mind had no idea what they were worth.

Kep made more stacks, placing the gold pieces in a separate pile. Jacques's sharp gaze followed his movements, but he said nothing.

When Kep had stacked every coin, he tried to guess what it was all worth. Hopefully, a lot, maybe a hundred dollars—or rather a hundred pounds.

"I would like to be the one to deliver the letter," Kep whispered, unsure how close by any patrols could be.

Jacques gave a hard stare and said nothing.

Kep gestured to the pile. "I'll pay you all of it."

"You don't know the area," Jacques said in a low voice. "You wouldn't know a deer path if you were on it. What are you really up to?"

Kep felt like he'd been punched in the gut. He didn't think he'd been that obvious. Nervously, he glanced quickly at the cave exit. How much did Jacques suspect?

"I want to show my dedication to the king. Completing this mission would mean a lot."

"Did General Burgoyne put you up to this?" Jacques said harshly. "Some sort of test?"

"Test? No!" Kep hadn't seen that coming. "Burgoyne has *no* idea. Please. If I finish the mission, maybe the king would even give me an award—or something." Kep had no idea what honors the King George III handed out. Knighthood? "It is my duty to serve."

"Quite the little Loyalist, aren't you?"

"I—" Kep blinked. "I think it's important to believe in a cause bigger than yourself."

That part was true.

"Thus you wish to pay for the right to deliver the letter. And having betrayed a trust to Burgoyne, I'm to disappear into the wilderness?"

Kep hoped Jacques's comment about disappearing into the wilderness meant Jacques was warming to the plan. "What did you do before the war? I mean before you became a messenger?"

"A fur trader."

"You could go back to doing that," Kep said eagerly.

"We're sticking to the plan."

"If this isn't enough money—" Panicked that his plan was crashing and burning, Kep yanked a telescope out of his haversack with one hand and the compass with the other. "You can have this stuff too!" He put them next to the stacks of coins and fished out his pocket watch. "And this too!"

"All that noise. Were you wanting to alert rebel patrols? To get me killed?" Jacques asked. "So you could steal the letter and get the hero's award from your king?"

"That's crazy!" Kep said. "I nearly got killed too!"

"Hmmm," Jacques said. "You wouldn't survive on your own long enough to deliver it."

"I'm willing to take that chance! If you're worried about Burgoyne being mad, don't be," Kep urged. "I'll report back that we got attacked—that's true. I'll say you were too injured to go on. Hey, I can say you got shot!"

An odd look crossed Jacques's face, but it passed almost as soon as it came. "I'm sure Burgoyne is already sufficiently impressed with your loyalty in volunteering to guide this mission. Keep your money."

Kep grew impatient to close the deal. "I can get more money if that's what you want."

Kep would agree to pay any sum. It would require a return trip to get the money from Annie, but safeguarding America was basically priceless.

Jacque held up a hand, looking grim. "Money is the only freedom. Learn to keep ahold of your money while you're young."

"I don't need it!" Kep eagerly grabbed up a handful of coins and pushed them toward Jacques. "No one needs to know. You told Burgoyne yourself that the king isn't your monarch. You're not even a Loyalist, right?"

Jacques went very still. Almost imperceptibly, his hand crept to his knife.

Kep swallowed anxiously. Clearly he'd touched a nerve "You just said money is freedom. Why *wouldn't* you just take the money?"

"You ask a lot of questions." Jacque's gaze flicked to the cave entrance. He seemed to be debating something.

A new thought popped into Kep's mind. Could *Jacques* also be playing a deeper game?

"It's true I need money," Jacques rubbed his temple, pausing before he spoke. "But I need a lot more than you're offering."

"I can get you more! I can get it by—soon!"

Jacques blew out a breath. "Not the kind of money I need."

"Try me."

Instead of offering a price, Jacques said. "What are you 14? 15-years-old?"

"Thirteen."

"Go home. War is horrible. Both sides try to convince you of the 'glory of the cause.' But it's just talk. And the ones talking aren't the ones taking bullets. Do you have a family?"

"Huh?" Kep said. "Yes, I have a family."

"Would you do anything for them?"

"Yes." Kep didn't hesitate. They were a big part of why he was risking his life in 1777. "I've got a brother. He was—shot. In the war. I was so scared for him. So scared he'd die." Kep's voice choked slightly.

"I have a sister." Jacques's voice took on a hard edge. "She lives at a fort, in Canada, with my two little nieces. She was recently widowed. The fort doesn't want more mouths to feed. The fort commander is pressuring her to marry a louse of a man."

"That's terrible!" Kep said. "Can't she leave?"

"She has nowhere to go. Besides, for a widow with young girls, the fort is safer. There is a small store at the fort. A widow could run such a business respectably. But she needs to pay the costs of the startup supplies. No one will offer credit to a woman."

"And Burgoyne is willing to pay a lot to get that letter through," Kep said, as a complicated situation just got more complicated. "How much more does she need?"

"A lot more than what's in your pile." Jacques gestured sharply to the money. "Time is ticking. I knew the English were paying couriers well – very well – because so many have been hanged. I am willing to gamble for the chance to keep her from that louse."

Kep's head pounded. He didn't want this sister to be forced to marry some horrible man either, but no way could Jacques deliver that letter.

"Just name your price. I can get it to you tomorrow."

Jacques gave him a wry, sad smile that said as plain as words he had no faith Kep was going to be producing big bucks anytime soon. And frankly, Kep had no way to prove to him otherwise.

Jacques moved toward the cave opening and listened. "It's quiet. We need to be going. This safehouse we're going to is along the banks of the river, so we'll follow that." He pointed toward the river, which could be seen in the distance. The moon glinted off the water. "I'll lead. Step light. We want you to live long enough to collect your British honors and for my sister and nieces to be saved from a life of misery."

Kep scrambled after him. His stomach felt as heavy as if it had a pile of rocks inside. He'd failed, once again at his mission to get ahold of the letter.

The odds Mary had found the note and the map and warned the rebels, who would be conveniently waiting at the safehouse, were a million to one. A zillion to one.

And he had to admit that the zillion to one chance also involved leading Jacques, who he was beginning to sympathize with, into an ambush.

Outside the cave, Jacques slid the rest of the way down the ravine, then began moving in the direction of the river. A fishy, weedy odor grew stronger.

Kep mimicked Jacques's movements and walked nearly as silently. Jacques looked back and gave him a nod of approval. When they reached the riverbank and followed it, the faint lapping water against the shore was the only sound.

A chill river dampness crept into Kep. His heart was in his boots. Things were a mess. He was no closer to knowing what was in the letter even as the historic battle of the century was forming up. And if Mary and Finn *were* out there trying to reach the safehouse, they risked getting attacked by the same party that had attacked him and Jacques.

There were so many puzzles, but now was not the time to unravel them. Now he needed to come up with one last plan.

Chapter 19

Loyalist Safehouse

Kep and Jacques arrived at the Loyalist safehouse, a ramshackle cabin surrounded by tall weeds, where they would deliver the letter. Overhead the moon had climbed ever higher in the sky. The wavering light of a candle could be seen through windows on either side of the door.

They stayed in the dark for several minutes studying the cabin and listening hard. A branch cracked somewhere in the woods. Kep froze.

Had they been followed?

Against all odds, had Mary somehow gotten the message about the letter through to the rebels and they were lying in wait?

A long silence followed in the woods.

No help was arriving. A feeling of cold desperation flooded Kep's veins.

After a period of silence, Jacques motioned for Kep to stay back, then slipped to the cabin. He softly knocked five times. Two rapid. Three slow.

When the door creaked open, Kep rushed to join Jacques and keep the letter close.

A man, presumably the Loyalist, had a tangled gray beard and torn coat. He let them in, then closed the door, pulling a wood bar down across it to latch it.

Smoldering embers and a pile of ashes sat in the fireplace. The grimy walls were smoke stained. Dirty dishes were piled by a bucket next to a small table with two chairs. The only light came from two candles on the table.

"I was told there'd be only one." The Loyalist didn't sound happy.

Jacques gave a casual shrug. "Burgoyne changed his mind."

"You've got the letter?" The Loyalist repeatedly licked his lips and spoke in jerky bursts. "Let me see it."

With a narrow-eyed glance at Kep, Jacques pulled a folded letter with a red wax seal from his coat pocket.

And there it was. Right in front of Kep. Burgoyne's letter. Capturing it might tip the balance in the Americans' favor, might undo whatever plans Fox had underway.

But now it was two against one.

Maybe Kep's best chance was to leave with Jacques, then find an excuse to double back. The ragged clothes made him hopeful the guy could be bribed. If not, at least the guy didn't look as strong as Jacques and he was old, maybe Kep could steal it from him. It was a slim hope, but all he had for now.

But instead of handing it over, Jacques placed it back into his pocket. Kep's confusion grew when Jacques sat in a rickety chair near the fireplace and jabbed an iron poker at the hearth as if intending to spark the embers back to a fire. "I could use something to drink before we go. It's been a long trip and there's much ahead of us."

"Ahead—but—we're leaving the letter here?" The question popped from Kep's quickly constricting throat and earned him a glare from Jacques.

Jacques shook his head. "This man will escort us to the next destination."

Next destination?

Kep's plan was quickly falling apart. Jacques, meanwhile, seemed in no hurry. "A bite to eat wouldn't hurt."

"I'm not here to feed you," snapped the Loyalist.

Jacque shrugged again. "A drink will be fine. The boy might like one as well."

"We will leave immediately," said the Loyalist. "There is no time for idleness."

Suddenly the pounding of horses' hooves came from outside the cabin.

Everyone froze. The Loyalist cursed. He snatched a rifle from over the fireplace and rushed to peer out a window. "Snuff the candles!"

Jacques, who'd sprung to his feet, used his thumb and finger to put out the flames.

Kep raced to the other window. Under the bright moon at least a dozen men, some carrying flaming torches and all wearing bandanas to hide their faces, gathered in front of the cabin.

"We know you've got one of Burgoyne's messengers in there. Send him out!" a voice shouted.

Kep didn't move, his heart thundered and his brain couldn't think fast enough.

The voice shouted again. "Send him out or we'll burn the place down!"

"My god, they'll do it!" The Loyalist jolted back. "Those rebels have torched more than one house."

Jacques took the man's place at the window, crouched down and peered out.

"We'll count to ten!" A voice shouted. "One!"

Jacques crouched lower.

Kep had a horrible, horrible feeling that "help" had arrived. Mary *had* gotten the message through. But it wasn't supposed to be like this! "Don't go out!" he said. "They could shoot you!"

"Two. Three." A bullet pinged off the chimney.

The voice rang out again. "You're surrounded. If you want to save your skins and your home, send the courier out. And tell him to bring whatever message he was carrying from Burgoyne or it'll be worse for all of you."

"They'll burn us alive!" said the Loyalist, panting.

Kep's panicked gaze swept the cabin. "Is there a cellar?"

The Loyalist shook his head. "They'd find us in minutes. Or the flames would."

Kep's heart squeezed. This was on him. He couldn't let Jacques go out there. "I'll take the letter!" Kep said breathlessly. "I'll bring it to them!"

"They aren't expecting y—" Jacques shook his head. "It's my mission to complete. No matter what happens. You two stay here!"

In two strides, Jacques was at the door, lifted the heavy wooden bar and swung open the door.

"Don't go!" Kep breathed.

But Jacques had already walked out of the cabin, his hands up.

The Loyalist scrambled to the door and dropped the bar back across, looking as frightened as a trapped animal. He rushed back to one window and Kep anxiously peered out the other.

"Step away from the cabin where we can see you!" came the demand.

Jacques walked slowly toward the men.

Kep watched, horrified.

Jacques stopped a few feet from them and said loudly. "I'm the one you want. Promise you'll let the others be."

"We promise nothing. Hand over the letter."

"I don't have it," said Jacques.

Jacques didn't care enough about the British cause to risk his life. Why wasn't he giving them the letter?

Hand it over! Just hand it over so they let you leave.

Jacques stood still in the light of the torches.

"Search him!" shouted the man

Another man snatched the pouch Jacques had been wearing. Then they checked Jacques pockets and clothes. "Nothing, sir!"

Wait! Jacques wasn't lying?

Kep looked over at the Loyalist, who was still peering out the window. Jacques hadn't given it to him, so it had to be hidden here somewhere. Kep darted from the window, searching the bare bones cabin. He'd bring it out and save Jacques!

As he frantically hunted, the same voice shouted, "Whoever you are inside, we have a message for you to bring back to your Burgoyne. This is what will happen to each and every future messenger!"

A single gunshot cracked.

His heart in his throat, Kep bolted back to the window.

In the moonlight, Jacques lurched a step, then crumpled to the ground.

Burgoyne's Native American Allies

Burgoyne intended to terrorize the Americans, proclaiming theatrically: "I have only to give stretch to the Indian Forces under my command, and they amount to thousands, to overthrow the harden'd Enemies of Great Britain...Devastation, famine, and every concomitant horror that a reluctant, but indispensable prosecution of military duty must occasion."

The threat backfired. As word of his proclamation spread throughout the frontier, militias began to form.

General Burgoyne addressing his Indian allies, mostly Iroquois.

MISSION NOTES CORPS OF KRONOS

Chapter 20

Mystery Grave

Kep rushed toward the door of the Loyalist's cabin. He grabbed the latch bar to shove it up.

"Open that door and *I'll* shoot you!" The Loyalist jerked his gun toward Kep. "We could be next!"

Kep recoiled from the barrel and backed away, his hands up.

A voice shouted from outside. "Tell Burgoyne we'll bury this one. Civilized like. But the next messenger's body will be on a pole for his pickets to find. Tories aren't welcome in these parts. You'd be wise to flee while you can."

Kep dashed to the other window. As if in a nightmare, he watched two masked men, hats pulled low, drag Jacques's lifeless body by the arms. Jacques's boots scraped across the dirt.

Vomit rose in Kep's throat.

This was his fault. He had told Mary to warn the rebels. To have them waiting.

He'd never thought through what would happen next.

Stupid.

Rash.

Deadly.

A third masked man followed Jacques's body. He carried two shovels.

Chills spread down Kep's spine.

These men had intended to kill Burgoyne's messenger all along. They'd even brought the tools to bury him.

Jacques had never stood a chance.

If Kep had carried out the letter. It would have been his body dragged across the dirt.

A shudder ran through him.

The men dragged Jacques's body toward the same creek Kep and Jacques had crossed. Soon they were out of Kep's line of sight. In the distance, metal scraped against stone.

"They'll come in here next!" The Loyalist looked around wild-eyed. "We've got to find that letter!"

Kep didn't know if the guy intended to hand it over to save their lives or hide it, but he wasn't about to argue. Kep and the Loyalist scoured the area where Jacques had sat, peering under the chair, searching the table, checking around the fireplace.

No letter.

"We need to escape." The Loyalist used a fireplace poker to pry boards away from the back of the house, making a hole in the frame.

Panic burrowed into Kep's gut. Would his body be the next one dragged to a shallow grave?

Kep rushed to help yank away boards, some rotted. Soon they'd made a hole big enough to squeeze through. The Loyalist scrambled through on his belly and Kep followed.

The house backed to thick woods. The Loyalist disappeared into them, running flat out along a narrow path. Kep did the same.

Kep's boots thudded against the ground. Branches scraped his shoulders.

He ran until his lungs felt they would burst. Wishing he could escape what he had seen. The Loyalist turned down another path, but Kep stopped.

He listened carefully. The woods were dark and cold and silent. There were no sounds of a chase.

He had no idea how far he'd run.

Feeling shaken, he leaned against a tree. The weight of all that had happened pulling him down, he sank to the forest floor.

Jacques had died. Men died during wars, but this was different. This time, Kep was the cause. His chest felt cold and empty.

The only way the rebels could have known Jacques would be at the safehouse is if Mary had found the note he'd left, identifying the Loyalist by name. She must have delivered that note to Mr. Banneker. And he'd given it to his rebel son or to some rebel group.

Jacque had done nothing to deserve this. He'd only agreed to deliver that letter to save his sister. Just like Kep was trying to do a job to save his country, save his family.

And for nothing.

Jacques had died.

The letter was gone.

Time was running out. Kep pulled out his pocket watch. 10:30 p.m. He'd told his parents he'd be home tonight and how desperately he wanted to be back with his family. Now.

But what if home wasn't there? Home might only exist if the American rebels won this battle. And winning might depend on that letter.

Kep played out the scene again in his head. He and that Loyalist had thoroughly searched the cabin. Jacques hadn't hidden it there. He had to have it on him. The rebel who'd checked his pockets had missed it. Or Jacques had a secret pocket or something. But somehow, Jacques had died still carrying that letter.

Kep circled back, quietly slipping along the path toward the cabin.

His entire mission. He couldn't let it be for nothing. He would get the letter and deliver it to the Americans.

When he neared the cabin, he stopped to listen.

An owl hooted in the distance. Otherwise, only silence. The rebels had gone.

Kep slowly approached the hole he and the Loyalist had escaped from to peer inside. Moonlight glimmered through smashed windows. The door lay on the floor, bashed off its hinges.

The table had been overturned and a chair broken into bits.

The rebels had clearly searched the place, but Kep was sure they hadn't found the letter.

There was only one place that the letter could be.

Dread made his insides feel heavy.

Finding the letter would take more than moonlight. Kep skirted the outside of the cabin and entered the cabin's open doorway. He grabbed a tipped over candle still in its pewter stand and held the wick to red embers glowing in the fireplace.

Once the candle caught flame, Kep went back outside. Goosebumps traveled down his spine as he followed along in Jacques's final footsteps.

He paused where Jacques had faced the rebels.

Dark splotches marked the grass where blood had oozed.

His stomach squeezed and he averted his eyes.

He clenched his fist, told himself to be strong and used every ounce of determination to keep walking.

Near the steep bank of the creek stood a fresh mound of dirt with rocks tossed over it.

Jacques's grave.

Hot tears streamed down Kep's cheeks. He angrily brushed them away. This was not the time. He closed his mind to everything but getting the letter. Finishing the mission.

He set the candle next to the edge of the steep bank that dropped to the creek and pulled off the heaviest rocks.

Be strong.

He shuddered but did not stop. Next, he dug his hands into the cold clumps of dirt, dreading the jolt of touching Jacques's body. Touching Jacques's still warm corpse.

He dug past his elbows. The smell of dirt filled his nose. Dirt jammed under his fingernails.

Suddenly, the dirt collapsed. Like some kind of sinkhole. Confused, he scooped dirt faster.

Surely the shallow grave wasn't deeper than Kep's arms. He searched for a sturdy branch. He found a four-foot one, stripped its side branches and walked up and down the mound, poking, but again and again, it only sunk into dirt.

Kep tried pushing the stick in at angles.

Suddenly, it slipped in extremely far, as if into an empty hole.

Kep scrambled to push away the dirt, grabbed the candle, and peered closer.

That was when he saw it.

An opening toward the creek.

He lay on his stomach, bending down and could feel the air and hear the creek babble.

There was no body.

The grave was empty.

Jacques was not dead.

Chapter 21
Arrested

Relief flooded through Kep.

Bewilderment followed.

Had Jacques faked his own death? Like they did in the movies? Or been knocked unconscious and come to in time to dig himself out? People buried alive in mudslides and avalanches sometimes clawed their way out.

He scrambled down the bank, across a thick patch of crunchy brown ferns and studied the opening.

The opening was just wide enough for a person to squeeze through. It led to the creekbank.

Kep stared while thoughts tumbled through his mind. Jacques still had the letter. The Loyalist was supposed to guide Jacque to some handoff point. But the Loyalist had long since fled to the woods. Even if Jacques went looking for him, the odds were slim he'd find the guy. And by himself, Jacques would have no idea where to take the letter. Not to mention, having been shot, he couldn't move quickly. Would Jacques give up his mission? Or...reconsider handing the letter over to Kep?

Hope rose in his chest. Kep glanced into the dark forest around the cabin. If only he could follow Jacques's trail.

But Kep was no tracker.

The grass in the immediate area had been trampled, but beyond that, there was no obvious trail to follow. Kep glanced back toward where he'd seen that dark puddle near the cabin and winced. He studied the ground but couldn't detect a path of blood. Nor were there muddy footprints or whatever a real tracker would follow.

A new thought occurred. Maybe Mary hadn't reached the Bannekers after all. Maybe the Bannekers hadn't passed along a message to the rebels about the locations of the Loyalist safehouse. Instead, the rebels might have simply tracked Kep and Jacques through the woods. And if they did it once, they probably could do it again.

One thing was clear. Kep couldn't succeed at this mission alone. He needed help. Help from people who shared his goal to protect America. Help from people trying to protect their fragile newly-forming nation.

The Bannekers family fit that definition. Their son, the one Parr had gone to their farm looking for, was a suspected rebel spy. He might have answers about Jacques. And the letter.

The thought of Parr made Kep shiver. If Mary hadn't reached the family to warn them, they still had no idea Parr intended a midnight raid at their farm.

Kep needed to reach the family ahead of Parr.

He dug into his haversack and yanked out the area map and his compass. Using the river's bend, which was near the Loyalist cabin, the bridge near the Banneker's farm and the location of his time portal as markers, he got his bearings.

He set off again, keeping his compass handy. He sped along in near silence. Jacques had taught him well. His throat tightened thinking of Jacques, hoping he was okay.

As Kep neared the bridge, he heard footsteps. He tucked behind the broad trunk of an oak and strained his ears. At this point, he was as freaked out about encountering gangs of rebels as redcoats.

The footsteps sounded like just one person. Whoever it was likely hadn't heard Kep, but he stayed crouched down to be safe.

In the moonlight Kep saw a girl with blond hair hurrying along the road.

A familiar girl.

"Mary!" Kep stepped from his hiding spot.

She whirled toward him, a hand to her throat. "Jesus, Mary and Joseph! Jumping out of the forest like some bandit!"

"Sorry!" Emotions swirled in Kep. It was good to see a familiar face, but his letter mission had failed. And he didn't know if the Banneker family would get out of this alive.

As she drew closer, he saw that she was more than simply scared. She was terrified.

Even back in Boston, when she had faced down an armed British guard, he'd never seen her so frightened. Her face was white.

"What's the matter?"

Mary grabbed his arm with icy fingers and a bruising tightness.

"Me brother..."

Kep swallowed, his throat suddenly dry.

'Is Finn—dead? Is that what you're trying to say?"

Blood pounded in his ears.

"Finn's been arrested!" Mary's eyes were bright with desperation. "They say—they say they'll hang him!"

Kep felt panic welling through his chest.

Be calm, he told himself. Panic will not help.

"What happened?" He asked as much to buy himself time to stop the rushing feeling of blood in his brain as to gather facts.

For a moment, her face crumpled as if she couldn't bear to tell the story. "Finn got it into his head to get the baroness's journal. To bring it to General Gates at the American camp." She gasped a shuddery breath. "T'was me own fault. I told him that you had tried and failed. He insisted he'd succeed."

Kep's anxiety skyrocketed. He tried to tell himself it was just for Finn's safety. But a small, okay large, part of his brain was yelping that Finn, his ancestor, needed to stay alive long enough to marry and have children for Kep to come into existence. Kep even knew the name of the woman Finn would one day marry. That is, if Finn didn't get himself hanged by Burgoyne first.

If his ancestor was dead—would he, Kep, disappear any moment?

"Me brother was inside the baroness's cabin when a watchman caught him. They say he was either trying to rob the baroness—" her voice got squeaky—"or that he planned to assassinate her husband, General Von Riedesel."

Yikes!

Kep tried to sound calm. "Where is he now?"

"They're keeping him in the camp prison. He's to have a court martial. They want to make an example." She took a shaky breath. "Ye'd asked me to warn the Bannekers. I was on my way there hoping to find you. To get your help. We must get Finn out!"

Get Finn out as in break him out? Of a jail smack dab in the middle of the British army camp?

"Right," Kep nodded with way more certainty than he felt. He was struggling to keep up with the crises exploding around him. Trying to piece together more of the puzzle, he asked, "So you didn't find the map of the Loyalist's cabin?"

"Map of the *Loyalist's* cabin?" She looked confused.

"The *other* map. The one I drew. On paper. I told you in the note that if I could find out the safehouse location, I'd leave you a map— the one I hid a map near Burgoyne's headquarters—"

Her fists clenched as if ready to clobber him.

"By *Burgoyne's headquarters*! Are ye thick in the head?" Mary spoke at an even higher pitch. "If ye put my name on it I'll be arrested by Burgoyne's soldiers the minute I step foot back in camp!"

"Of course, I didn't put your name on it!" How stupid did she think he was? Kep took a deep breath to steady his nerves. "When is the trial— er court martial?"

"In three days." Her voice trembled. "They'll find him guilty, Kep. They *want* to find him guilty!"

"We will get him out, but we can't do it alone." Kep desperately tried to think who would be willing and able to aid in a prison break. To save Finn. To save history. Who could travel into a British camp without being identified as rebels or rebel sympathizers?

Tela, TJ, and Max. He would need his team. But he'd have to travel back to get them. "I can get help, but we can't get him out tonight."

Her shoulders dropped.

Kep suspected she was holding back tears and wished they could break Finn out now, tonight, but it wasn't possible. They couldn't do it alone.

"Did ye get the letter from the courier?" Mary finally asked. "To give to General Gates."

"No." Kep quickly told her the story. The Loyalist cabin. The attack. Jacques's empty grave.

"'Tis mysterious." She chewed her lip. "Time is growing short. If Burgoyne succeeds in getting past Gate's army and marches into Albany, 'tis all over. The town is seething with Tories and they'll hand it to him on a serving trencher. These blasted British already hold New York town."

"The Americans have got to stop Burgoyne here," Kep agreed.

"And the Banneker family have not been warned of that horrid Parr coming tonight." Her eyes widened. "Could Parr have already done his evil deeds?"

Kep didn't want to think about that. "I was just going that way." He pulled out his pocket watch. Parr's midnight visit loomed closer.

"We *will* get Finn out somehow before the trial," Kep said. "Right now we've got to warn the Bannekers. And see if they can help track down that letter."

Kep took off across the bridge and Mary followed.

"I'll be going with ye. If I can help save one person from those horrid British, me soul will rest easier. One day the invaders shall melt off the earth like snow off a ditch!"

Joseph Brant

Joseph Brant was a Mohawk military and political leader associated with Great Britain during the American Revolution. He met many significant people of the age, including both George Washington and King George III.

Brant saw the Crown's presence as a safeguard against colonial incursions into Native American land. While still in his teens, Brant led war parties against the French during the Seven Years' War. During the revolution, Brant led Mohawk and colonial Loyalists known as "Brant's Volunteers" against the rebels on the New York frontier. He was accused by the Americans of committing atrocities and given the name "Monster Brant", but the accusations were argued by later historians to have been false.

After the war, Chief Brant relocated with most of his people to Upper Canada to the area which is now Six Nations Reserve.

Thayendanegea or Chief Joseph Brant

Chapter 22
Trust

Kep and Mary raced down the road toward the Banneker's farmhouse. The wind grew colder, but Kep's leg muscles burned. They had to warn the Bannekers about Parr's raid. And find out any possible information about Jacques. With every passing hour, Jacques and the letter would become harder to track.

Pops of scattered gunshots sounded. They crashed to a halt then ducked into the underbrush at the side of the road.

Kep crouched beside Mary, his heart racing.

"Patrols?" Mary whispered.

"Probably. Jacques and I barely made it to that Loyalist cabin." The no-man's land between two warring armies was extremely dangerous.

At least the shots sounded a way off. When it was quiet again, Kep and Mary cautiously started back down the road.

In a field near the Banneker's farm, cornstalks rustled in the breeze. Kep and Mary approached carefully, darting behind a chicken coop to scout the area.

From inside the coop, a sudden *baak-bak-bak-bak* sounded. Maybe Henny, the chicken that redcoat had tried to steal, had heard them. Kep put a finger to his lips and poked his head around to look toward the house.

No sign of Parr or his men. Kep sagged with relief.

The house was dark, but smoke puffed from the chimney.

"We'd best be warning them what's to come." Mary led the way across the grass.

Shutters had been pulled over the windows hiding any sign of movement inside. The family was likely sleeping peacefully, with no idea the danger that this night held.

The last time the Bannekers had seen him, Kep had gone riding off with the same British gang that had terrorized their family. His welcome far from certain, he knocked nervously.

No one answered.

He drummed harder on the door.

"Perchance they've left," whispered Mary. "Or...Captain Parr has been here ahead of us. Arrested them? Or worse?"

Nerves fluttered in his stomach. Kep twisted the door handle and pushed, but the door was barred.

Mary grabbed his arm. "Did ye hear that footstep? Someone's inside."

Kep eyed a window as a possible entrance.

"Who's there?" An elderly man's gruff voice barked from inside.

"You've got to get out of here." Kep spit out the words as fast as he could.

The door swung open and Kep stumbled back as a rifle barrel trained on him.

Mr. Banneker peered out, shoving a lantern toward their faces. "What do you want?" he barked. "You were here—"

"The British officer, Captain Parr," Kep broke in. "He's coming back. Midnight tonight!"

Mr. Banneker stilled. From behind him, Juba rushed up with her two enormous dogs.

"They'll find the man!" she cried.

"Hush child!" Mr. Banneker said sharply.

Kep and Mary exchanged a glance.

"What man?" Kep asked Juba. Parr had come searching for Juba's father as a suspected spy. But Juba wouldn't refer to her father as "the man."

Juba grabbed her grandpa's hand as her words tumbled out. "He's too badly hurt! He can't run."

Too badly hurt. Blood rushed to Kep's ears as he tried to make sense of this. "Jacque is *here*? You—caught him?"

One of the dogs gave a deep warning bark at Kep's outburst.

"Jesus, Mary and Joseph," Mary said under her breath.

"We didn't *catch* him." Juba laid a hand on the dog's head. "We're *helping* him."

Kep's mind was spinning. Had Jacques convinced this rebel family he was just some injured man needing assistance?

"Juba! Out!" Mr. Banneker ordered. But Juba only backed up a few paces.

"Jacques is a *British messenger*! Where do you have him?" Kep instinctively stepped forward, but the dogs' low growl stopped him in his tracks.

Mr. Banneker didn't budge. More confusing, he looked neither appalled nor astonished at the news about Jacques. "Loyalists are not welcome here. You'd best be on your way."

"I'm *not* a Loyalist!" Kep insisted. "But Jacques *is* working for the British!"

What part did Mr. Banneker not understand?

Mr. Banneker moved to slam the door, and Mary dashed forward. "We'd not be here warning ye of Captain Parr's arrival if we were Loyalists."

"Who would you be?" Mr. Banneker jerked his head toward Mary.

"I canna say," Mary replied. "Trust there is no true Irish on the side of the bloody British so you needn't be worrying on that account. Yet ye and your family are in great danger."

"We've got to move him before those soldiers come back!" Juba pleaded with her grandfather.

Kep had no idea why they would be hiding Jacques, but he wasn't about to leave.

"We can help." *And find out about the letter.* "We'll help move Jacques. You've got to get out!"

"Ye'd be the only one with a gun," Mary said. "We'd be meaning you no harm."

A host of emotions crisscrossed Mr. Banneker's face, but he stepped aside to let Kep and Mary enter. "If you're lying, you'll regret it."

Chapter 23
Secrets Revealed

Kep and Mary stepped inside the Banneker's farmhouse into a room with herbs hanging from the ceiling beams, a large spinning wheel and a crackling fire in a stone fireplace. An iron tea kettle hung over the flames, puffing steam. The dogs remained on either side of Juba, her personal sentries, and Kep and Mary kept a respectful distance.

Mr. Banneker led them along a narrow hallway, still holding his rifle and looking grim. He opened the door to a small, dimly lit room.

In the yellow light of candles, Mrs. Banneker bent over a bed bandaging a man's ankle. She looked up, startled. "Why would you bring someone—" She blinked at Kep. "You!"

But Kep's entire focus was on the man sitting on the bed. A man whose face was scratched, his lip swollen with a cut, and his clothes caked in mud.

Even though he'd figured out the identity of "the man," Kep couldn't help a jolt of relief. "Jacques!"

Jacques's mouth fell open and his hand shot to a knife at his belt. "How did you find me?" Without waiting for an answer, he shouted to Mr. Banneker, "Get him out! He's with Burgoyne!"

"*You're* with Burgoyne!" Kep blurted, his mind reeling.

"What's going on?" Mr. Banneker jerked his head at Jacques. "How does this boy fit in?" His hand tightened on his rifle and he levied a glare at Kep and Jacques. "You'd best explain yourselves."

Kep began to reiterate that Jacques was the one working for the British, but he bit his tongue. That news didn't seem to surprise Mr. Banneker at the door moments earlier. Something more was going on.

Jacques's eyes darted around the room. When he spoke again, his pace was slow as if choosing his words carefully. "The boy, Kep, was sent to accompany me to the safehouse—by General Burgoyne." Jacques exhaled. "If I'm found out, they'll slit my throat."

It was an odd choice of words. Militaries don't slit throats. But Jacques did look terrified.

Mr. Banneker turned his hard stare on Kep.

"I did it to spy. I'm on the American side," insisted Kep.

Jacques's eyebrows shot up.

"I was spying on Burgoyne—no time to explain it all. One of Burgoyne's officers, Captain Parr, he's on his way!"

"Coming *here*?" Jacques struggled to rise, but his half-bandaged, grotesquely-swollen ankle gave out and he fell back on the bed. "I have to get out!"

"When?" Mrs. Banneker asked breathlessly.

"Midnight," Kep replied.

"They mustn't find him here!" Mrs. Banneker said.

"We can hide you in the smokehouse," Mr. Banneker said to Jacques.

"They could search there," insisted Mrs. Banneker. "The cornfield?"

"They've burned more than one field."

"The old Smith place has been abandoned for months. We could hide in the ice house." Mrs. Banneker looked at Kep and Mary. "Can you help move him across the pasture?"

"Tell me what's going on first." Kep stared at Jacques. "How did you get away from the rebels? Why're you here?"

"Get my boots!" was Jacques's only answer.

"Your foot is too swollen," Mrs. Banneker said.

"We need their help to move you. The boy claims to be on the rebel side," said Mr. Banneker to Jacques. "The fact he and the girl are here to warn us supports that."

"Unless you can hop or crawl fast enough to escape, you won't get far without our help," Kep warned.

Jacques narrowed his eyes at Kep. "You claim you were *pretending* to be on the British side. Then why did you want to deliver the letter so badly?"

"To get it to the American General Gates," Kep answered honestly.

"*He's* going to deliver a letter to Gates!" Juba pointed to Jacques. "But he needs Papa's help."

What the heck?

"Juba! Hush your babble!" Mr. Banneker snapped. "Out now!"

Juba pursed her lips tightly, as if holding back a load of arguments. She dragged her feet as she left the room, her dogs at her heels.

Mr. Banneker shut the door behind her.

"You...changed sides? To the rebels?" Kep asked Jacques, trying to process this new information.

Something flickered in Jacques's eyes, then it was gone.

Mr. Banneker snorted. "He's on the side of gold currency. The Americans are paying a fortune for the letter."

Jacques had planned to hand over the letter all along?

The logic suddenly fell into place. Jacques had no loyalty to the British. He'd angrily told General Burgoyne that King George III wasn't his sovereign. Jacques needed money, a boat load of it to save his sister. If Burgoyne was willing to pay a "fortune," Burgoyne's own words, for Jacques to deliver the letter, how much more would the rebels pay to get their hands on it. A thread of grudging admiration shot through Kep. It was—kind of genius.

The worst part was that Kep had nearly undone Jacques's plan.

"But—they *shot* you!" Kep stared at a dark red stain on Jacques's coat. "The blood-"

"Chicken blood. I kept it in a pouch," Jacques said coolly. "The killing was a ruse."

"'Twas all planned?" Mary looked as shocked as Kep felt. "Ye'd be playing a double role all along? And the rebels were knowing—the entire mission?"

Jacques nodded. "Yes."

Kep's brain was exploding and he shook his head to clear it.

"I was to turn it over to a second courier and couldn't risk Burgoyne suspecting that I had turned it over to the rebels. If he knew, he'd hunt me down the same as other couriers who'd changed sides. He couldn't know I was still alive," said Jacques.

"So ye tipped off the rebels to where you'd be," Mary said.

"But—they searched you." Kep's head was spinning. "And they searched the cabin."

"Part of the show," said Jacques grimly.

"But if it was all planned, why not just give them the letter to deliver to General Gates themselves?"

Jacques barked a harsh laugh. "That's what they wanted. But I must deliver the letter." He grimaced. "I was to go to the American camp on foot after the—incident—at the safehouse. But I twisted my foot scrambling down an embankment."

Kep had a hundred questions but narrowed it down to the most critical. "Do you still have the letter?"

Jacques hesitated. "Yes."

"I'll take it to the Americans! Just give me directions to their camp." Kep held out his hand, relieved by how things had turned out. He'd deliver the letter to General Gates, thwarting whatever plot Fox and Burgoyne had dreamed up, then return home. Mission complete!

"No!" Jacques sat straighter on the bed. "You'd never make it. We barely made it to the safehouse. Another rebel group could ambush you."

Mr. Banneker nodded gravely. "The woods are crawling with advance scouts and rebel groups. Burgoyne may strike at any time. They are watching hawklike. Any movement in the woods could be Burgoyne's advance scouts. They'd as soon shoot a man as a rabbit and ask questions later."

"But you're injured. I've got two good legs!" insisted Kep.

"If you're shot before you can explain what you're doing, the entire mission is lost," Jacques insisted. "Mr. Banneker's son knows the rebels well. He'll be here soon with a horse. He'll escort me."

"Horseback will be much faster than on foot," added Mr. Banneker.

"I can ride!" Kep argued. "If you're worried about—being paid, I'll make sure they know I got the letter from you."

Jacques stiffened. "The letter must be delivered by me, not some boy. So that American General Gates knows it has never left my person and that it is exactly what Burgoyne wrote."

"But even with an escort, you might not make it!" Kep wanted to kick something, but he forced himself to focus on a plan b. "At least let us read the letter. Then if you don't make it, one of us can get the message verbally to General Gates."

Jacques shook his head. "It's sealed. And must remain so."

Kep wanted to scream. Jacques had to have the letter hidden on him, but short of tackling the guy and physically taking it, Kep had no way to get it. Kep's eye shot from Mr. Banneker's rifle to the hunting knife at Jacques's waist belt. He suspected he'd come out second if he tried to attack. There was no doubt that Jacques being the one to deliver it would carry more weight with General Gates. And it was true that he and Jacques had barely made it to the Loyalist safehouse alive. But if Jacques were captured, Kep, and more importantly, General Gates, would never know what was in the letter.

"This arguing is wasting time. The main thing right now is getting Jacques moved," urged Mr. Banneker. "Whatever foul plans this Captain Parr intends, none of us can remain here."

Lord Dunmore's Proclamation

Lord Dunmore's Proclamation (1775)

John Murray, Earl of Dunmore

Lord Dunmore's proclamation in 1775 promised freedom to any indentured servants and enslaved African Americans held in bondage by American revolutionaries, so long as they were willing to bear arms for British troops fighting against American forces during the Revolutionary War.

Chapter 24

Escape Plans

Mrs. Banneker rapidly tore the final strips of linen and finished wrapping Jacque's foot and ankle.

Kep took deep calming breaths through his nose. He and Mary couldn't carry a 180-pound, six-foot man. And Jacques, with his broken ankle or foot, could hardly hop across an entire pasture to hide in some icehouse. "How do we move him?"

"We can put him in my cart!" Juba burst into the room. Likely she'd been listening at the door. "Patriot and Liberty can pull him!" She put a hand on each of her two dogs' heads.

"Absolutely not!" said Mrs. Banneker. "I won't have you shot by a stray bullet."

"If ye'd be having a dog cart, why not use it to take him to the American camp?" asked Mary.

Mr. Banneker shook his head. "It's too slow and creates a lot of noise. We still need a fast horse and Juba's dad to accompany Jacques. We could use the cart to get him to the Smith's old farm through."

"Juba will *not* be a part of this!" Mrs. Banneker snapped at her husband.

"With Captain Parr coming, it's more dangerous for her to be here," said Mr. Banneker. "You can't drive the cart and I need to head off our son so he doesn't come back here and blunder into that British gang."

"What can we be doing to help?" asked Mary.

"You two," Jacques looked from Mary to Kep, "could stall Captain Parr. Give us time to get away."

Kep blinked. "Stall him how?" His mind shot to how many guns and soldiers were in Parr's gang of thugs. Then he remembered something from his mission notes. "Maybe we could create some kind of roadblock? When Burgoyne's army marched from Canada, the rebels slowed them by piling brush and cutting trees to fall across the roads."

"That took dozens of men, working day and night with axes and pry bars," Mr. Banneker said. "Besides, such a roadblock only slows wagons. A small group of men on horseback can easily get around it."

Kep's face flushed. Mr. Banneker was right.

"We could be sprinkling holy water in their path, the devils," muttered Mary.

"They have to cross the bridge to get here." Mrs. Banneker looked thoughtful. "That might be the key."

"Are you saying destroy the bridge?" Kep said.

"Yes."

"Might they not get around it some other way?" Mary asked.

Mrs. Banneker shook her head. "The gorge beneath is too steep to take horses down."

"Might they use a different bridge?"

"The other is miles away," Mrs. Banneker said. "It would give us time."

"Wouldn't they be suspecting the destroyed bridge was your doing?" Mary said. "Captain Parr is already bent on some evil mission. If it's found out about the bridge, mightn't that bring even more trouble from the British?"

"They don't know you've warned us," said Mrs. Banneker. "Besides, rebels have already destroyed a number of bridges in the area. There would be nothing to tie it to us if it was done right."

"Done right?" Kep asked. "How?"

The clock was ticking. An immediate solution was desperately needed, but no one had an answer. Until...

"We could drop a tree across the bridge!" Kep said.

Mr. Banneker shook his head. "Cutting down a large tree takes time and a lot of skill to predict which way it will fall."

"What about taking the bridge planks up?" Kep said. "We could rip out the first part. It would be impassable, and no one would know who did it!"

Mr. Banneker shook his head again. "Not enough time."

"Burn it," offered Jacques.

"It's been damp. The wood isn't likely to start fire," said Mrs. Banneker.

"We'd need something combustible – something that would burn hot enough to start the beams." Mary said slowly. "Gunpowder might do the trick."

Mr. Banneker frowned. "Gunpowder is extremely dangerous."

"Other ideas?" Kep looked around the room hopefully.

Crickets.

Kep shrugged. "I think it's our only option."

"Juba, show them where we keep the gunpowder. I'll get the cart ready." Mr. Banneker handed her the lantern, grabbed one of the remaining candles, and shuffled quickly out of the room, calling Juba's dogs to follow. "Patriot. Liberty. Come here!"

Juba hurried out after him with Kep and Mary at her heels.

When Mr. Banneker turned toward the barn, Juba led them to a cowshed.

Mary held out an arm to slow Kep as Juba rushed ahead and whispered, "Can we be sure Jacques's story isn't blarney?"

Kep wondered as well. There seemed something naggingly odd about Jacque's insistence on taking the letter himself. Or maybe being a spy himself had made Kep extra distrustful. There was some logic to Jacques's story. Jacques desperately needed money, assuming the story about his sister was true.

"It's not like Juba's dad is taking him anywhere else than to the American camp," Kep said. "And he is motivated by money. Still, it would be great to see the actual letter."

"I may have an idea," Mary said quietly.

"What?"

"Let me see if it'll work first."

Juba was already inside the empty cowshed when they caught up with her. The smell of manure and straw was strong.

"We took Bessy and her calf to Aunt Sarah's. Papa said the British will steal them if they find them. Uncle Jesse is keeping his chickens hidden in the root cellar." Juba lifted a board to expose a wooden box hidden beneath. "We had to hide a bunch of stuff when the British came."

"For a wee one, you know many secrets." Mary said. "I bet you even know where that man, Jacques, would be hiding the letter that your papa is helping him bring to the Americans."

Juba nodded and Kep's heart skipped a beat.

"He showed it to Papa. The man, Mr. Jacques, made me leave the room first, but I watched through the crack under the door," Juba offered proudly. "Papa wanted to take the letter to General Gates himself, just like you did." She glanced at Kep. "But Mr. Jacques said it would wreck the whole plan. He threatened to eat it." Juba giggled, then turned serious. "And he had his hand on that knife at his belt. That wasn't nice of him."

Juba looked from Kep to Mary and lowered her voice dramatically, clearly enjoying having their full attention. "And there's *another* secret!"

"Let's just focus on that first secret," Kep said. "Where is the letter?"

Juba looked annoyed at having her second secret brushed aside.

"I'd love to be knowing either secret." Mary shot a sharp look at Kep to shut up.

"I'll tell just you," Juba said to Mary, then shot a pointed look at Kep and used her fingers to gesture him away.

Kep stepped back, annoyed at upsetting the key witness, so to speak.

Juba cupped her hands and stood on tip toe to whisper into Mary's ear.

Mary grimaced as she listened.

Juba finished and crossed her arms, her chest puffed up.

"That's quite a secret indeed," Mary said. "Can you tell us where the letter would be now?"

"Should I say in front of *him*?" Juba jerked a thumb toward Kep. She clearly held a grudge.

"T'would be best," Mary said. "We'd both be appreciating it."

Kep wisely kept his mouth shut.

"It's hidden in his boot. The one he had to take off because of his swollen foot. In a sort of pocket inside."

Knowing the contents of the letter would be insurance. If Jacques didn't make it to the Americans with the message, Kep could at least get a verbal summary to General Gates.

"Let's get Jacques loaded onto the wagon then," said Mary striding back toward the house. Kep tucked the box of gunpowder under one arm and followed her. He was going to get that letter.

"I'll help Grandpa harness Liberty and Patriot!" Juba dashed off toward the barn.

Kep quickly filled Mary in on his new plan. "I need to read that letter, but it can't be obvious that it's been opened. It's probably got a seal."

"They've a fire burning in the front room." She pursed her lips. "You could heat it and scrape it off, very gentle like. Then once you've read it, heat it just enough to press it back."

"I'll try. Is the 'second secret' more to worry about?"

Mary shook her head. "Something was stolen by the British, but she doesn't know what it is, so let's not trouble about it now."

Kep set the wooden box of gunpowder on the ground, ready to take it to the bridge as soon as Mr. Banneker had the cart ready and they had moved Jacques.

"We'll need a distraction." Mary laid out her plan and Kep agreed.

Chapter 25
The Letter

Back in the dimly lit room, Mrs. Banneker was helping Jacques put his coat back on. Kep spotted the brown leather boot near the bed. He moved near it and gave a tiny nod at Mary who'd positioned herself near the window.

"Jesus, Mary, and Joseph!' she exclaimed in shrill tones. "Something is moving out there. I'll douse the candle!"

She rushed to the small chest where the single candlestick stood and used her thumb and finger to snuff the flame and plunge the room into darkness.

A bitter smell of smoke wafted through the air. Before their eyes could adjust to the dark, Kep slipped his fingers into the boot, feeling for the pocket Juba had told them about. He felt the paper, pulled it out and tucked it under his shirt.

Mary dashed back to the window where Mrs. Banneker now stood pressing her face close to the glass, straining to see into the shadows outside.

Jacques lunged from the bed, but his ankle collapsed and he fell back.

"'Twould be safer to cover the window lest they see movement," Mary urged. She reached in front of Mrs. Banneker and yanked the curtain, blocking the moonlight and plunging the room deeper into darkness.

"Is it Parr's men?" demanded Jacques.

"I didn't see anyone," said Mrs. Banneker.

"Shove that trunk in front of the door!" ordered Jacques. "And the chair!"

Perfect. Just enough commotion to cover some time.

Mary hopped into action, dragging a chair across the wooden floor.

"Juba is at the barn with John. I need to warn them just in case." Mrs. Banneker pushed past Mary and out of the bedroom.

"You do that! I'll check out the front!" Kep rushed out of the room.

Kep dashed to the fireplace where the tea kettle hung on a metal hook. The hearth fire snapped. Kep held up the folded letter to its light. On the back was a red wax seal imprinted with a B.

Kep held the letter's seal over the spout of the teapot. Not enough steam. He grabbed an apron off a peg and used it to lift the teapot lid. More steam escaped and Kep held the back of the seal closer.

The wax softened slightly. But it was starting to melt!

He needed the heat under the seal directly.

Kep snatched his hunting knife from his haversack. He held its blade to the fire.

Then hand trembling ever so slightly, he gently slid the heated knife to the edge of the seal.

From the back room, Mary called in a low voice, "Kep, would ye be seeing anything from the front window?"

"I don't see anything yet," he called back. "But I'll keep an eye out for a few more minutes to be sure. Don't light that candle until I give the okay."

Kep forced his mind to focus. Everything was riding on him doing this just right.

He nudged and slid the knife farther under the seal. The heat of the metal allowed it to slide under the wax. A moment later, like a magic trick, it peeled off in one piece.

Gently placing the wax seal on the table by the fireplace, he quickly unfolded the letter, holding it to the light of the fire to read.

A short message. Three lines.

St. Ledger,

Sir, the battle date has now been set. We shall commence our attacks October 7. You shall lead your army to attack from the American rear and our army will attack their front. Victory will be ours.

General Burgoyne

Kep stared at the bold, swirling signature.

He rubbed his eye sockets as if it could change the words. But the message remained. By the time he finished, his heart was in his throat.

"Oh no! Oh no! Oh no!" he breathed. "*That* is why Burgoyne is so cocky!"

Fox *had* changed history.

American General Gates wouldn't be facing just *one* British army. A *second* British army was sneaking up on his rear.

If the scheme succeeded, it would be a game-changer. A history-changer. The odds of an American victory at Saratoga would plummet. And the attack would start in just four short days! General Gates needed to know about this plan. But he'd never believe it without seeing it with his own eyes. In Burgoyne's own handwriting. Signed. Sealed. Delivered by Burgoyne's own messenger.

Jacques needed to be the one to deliver that letter.

"Kep! Would ye be seeing anyone moving about?" called Mary.

"I think I may have! Quiet!" Kep called back.

His fingers ice cold, he refolded the letter. The next step was crucial.

He quickly heated the knife again, then picked up the wax seal he'd carefully scraped off and placed it on the knife. When the back softened a minuscule amount, he lifted it and gently pressed it to the letter fold.

The heated wax stuck onto the paper.

Success!

Kep tucked the letter back under his shirt and raced to the back room. "All clear. Maybe it was just an animal moving around in the dark."

"Thank the heavens." There was the sound of scraping furniture as Mary cleared the doorway from inside.

The door opened and Kep gave Mary the faintest of nods.

"I'll light the candle," Mary tripped over a chair she had just moved and cried out as she fell to the floor in the shadowy room near the bed.

Kep used this extra distraction to tuck the letter back into Jacques's boot.

"Are you okay?" he rushed to help Mary from the floor.

Getting to her feet, Mary lit the candle and in the flickering light, Jacques was strapping a small wood piece to his ankle as a brace.

A moment later Mrs. Banneker returned, her face lined. "The cart's ready. Hurry!"

Despite his swollen ankle, Jacques insisted on putting his boot back on. A grimace of pain crossed his face as he tugged and tugged. Thanks to Mary, Kep had read the letter just in time.

With the homemade brace, there was no way the boot would fit.

Jacques yanked the knife out of his belt and sliced the boot down the side enough to squeeze it over his foot.

Once he had his boot on, Jacques put his arms over Kep and Mary's shoulders and hopped out of the room and out of the house using his good leg.

Kep glanced back at the house. If Parr made it here and found the family gone but the coals in the fireplace still hot, he might well guess they were hiding nearby. All the more reason Kep and Mary had to succeed in stopping him.

Outside, Juba's dogs, Patriot and Liberty, were harnessed to a small cart. Juba sat on the driver's bench, holding the reins and looking determined.

They loaded Jacques onto the back of the cart. His feet hung over the edge and his face showed the pain that even the short trip to the cart had cost him.

Mrs. Banneker came out of the house with a basket of clattering glass bottles. "Oil. It'll help with the fire."

Mary took the basket and shoved a handkerchief between the glass bottles.

"I'll intercept Juba's father and direct him to the Smith's." Looking grim, Mr. Banneker handed his rifle to Jacques. "Keep a sharp lookout."

"We'll be waiting at their icehouse," Mrs. Banneker said.

Kep looked from Jacques to Juba, to Mr. and Mrs. Banneker. It wasn't his original team, but each person had a critical role to play in their mission to get the letter to General Gates. A new team, a team working together. "Good luck to everyone."

Mr. Banneker nodded. "Godspeed to us all."

They would head in three different directions. Mary and Kep would travel back to the bridge and destroy it, holding back Parr and his men. That would buy time for Mr. Banneker to find his son and send him to the icehouse at the abandoned farm's icehouse where Juba and her grandmother were taking Jacques. Then Juba's dad would accompany Jacques to deliver the critical letter to the American camp.

Juba said something to the dogs and they pulled and strained. The cart's wheels turned and Mrs. Banneker hobbled alongside, using one hand to hold onto the cart.

Mr. Banneker took off in another direction to intercept his son.

Kep picked up the box of gunpowder determined to keep Parr away long enough for Juba's dad to escort Jacques safely to the American camp, to slow Parr down to buy time or better yet keep him away altogether.

Mary shot a look at Kep. "We'd best be getting that bridge gone!"

The Battle of Bennington

Desperate for supplies, Burgoyne needed to replenish his forces. When he learned of supplies in lightly-defended Bennington, Vermont, he sent British, Loyalist, and Native American forces toward Bennington under the leadership of Lt. Col. Friedrich Baum to take them.

Local militia units discovered Baum's movements and under American Gen. John Stark began to prepare. Stark sent spies to Baum's camp claiming to be Loyalist recruits. They took a loyalty oath, but their real aim was to gather intelligence.

When Baum learned of Americans forces at Bennington, he sent couriers to Burgoyne asking for reinforcements stating that "uncouth militia" had gathered to stop him. Unfortunately for Baum, his reinforcements arrived just after the battle.

John Stark

Chapter 26

Demolition

Kep and Mary ran back down the narrow dirt road toward the bridge. A damp wind gusted their faces.

Kep clung to the wooden box of gunpowder, feeling jittery about the mission ahead.

The plan was to spread a layer of gun powder over the bridge beams then light it. Kep imagined it would be like pouring lighter fluid on a charcoal grill with the hope the resulting flames would catch the wood on fire. But would anything burn in this wet weather? How long since the last rain and how wet would that bridge be?

"What did ye learn from the letter?" Mary panted as she ran.

I learned Fox is about to destroy the country.

He kept that bad news to himself. Mary didn't know who Fox was. Didn't know Kep's grandfather had time-traveled over two hundred years to 1777 to destroy the United States at its birth. And this wasn't the time to spin that tale.

"St. Ledger is coming to flank the patriots," Kep said grimly.

"St. Ledger!" Mary stumbled and caught herself. "But he was turned back at Oriskany. By our brave General Arnold."

Our brave General Arnold? The biggest traitor in American history, who would conspire to hand over West Point to the British in two years' time.

Despite a twinge of guilt about keeping so much information from her, he simply said, "I don't know how things changed."

"But how will the Americans stand against *two* British armies?" Mary's breath became more labored as she ran.

"At least the letter will make sure General Gates knows what's ahead. The double attack won't come as a surprise."

It was critical they blocked Parr and his gang from crossing the bridge and finding Jacques before he delivered that letter.

Mary slowed, holding her side. "I've a stitch. Go on ahead."

Kep ran ahead, lengthening his stride, determined to beat Parr to the bridge.

Burning a bridge. Simple. In theory. For a professional arsonist on a calm night. Not so easy for an amateur in the dead of night, a windy night at that.

Soon he could see the bridge, which shot straight across the gully. He ran halfway across, skidded to a halt, and set down the gunpowder box.

His first clue of trouble occurred when he had to sweep away a thick layer of soggy leaves to get to the planks underneath.

Nervously, he ran his hand along the wood.

Damp.

With a feeling of dread, he scrabbled a few feet, shoved aside another pile of leaves and felt the wood again.

Even damper.

Between the fog earlier in the day, the blanket of moist leaves, and likely rain a day or two ago—his mind shot to the muddy puddles at the British camp—the wood was waterlogged.

His insides felt hollow.

Wet wood doesn't burn.

Even if they spread the gunpowder and lit it, the beams would never catch fire long enough to burn. Like pouring gasoline on a wet log – only the gas would burn.

Instinctively, he looked down the dark road toward the British camp.

Time was running out.

Mary arrived still clutching the basket of oil bottles.

"The planks are practically soaked," Kep blurted. "They'll never burn."

She dropped the basket with its clanking glass bottles and crouched to touch the wood. "Enough smoke might be holding them back. If we could get dry twigs from the woods and start enough leaves smoldering?"

"But how long till they burn out? Or the wind takes the smoke away?" There *had* to be a way to destroy the bridge.

His eyes fell on the box of gunpowder. "Could we—blow it up?"

Mary looked up and down the bridge. "The explosion would have to come from underneath. Back in Boston, the roof of a building was blown off by a gunpowder accident. If we could light the charge under it, the blast would destroy the planks. We'd have to direct the force at the weak points of the bridge."

Kep nodded. Glad his explosion partner had more knowledge than he did. She and Finn had once built a submarine to attack British ships in the Boston harbor. He wouldn't be shocked if they'd planned to attach some explosives to those ships. But this wasn't the time to ask.

In unison, they raced to the side of the bridge and lay on their stomachs to look beneath.

"The ground is over twenty feet down. We've not enough gunpowder for an explosion big enough to impact that far," Mary said.

Kep studied the underside of the bridge for someplace to wedge the wooden box. But there was no handy shelf. No set of trellises to set it on. "I've got a rope. Maybe it's long enough to hang the box underneath?"

Kep quickly uncoiled the rope he'd stolen, or rather bought since he left the coins, for his original plan to tie up "the messenger."

But it wasn't even ten feet. His shoulders slumped.

Mary looked toward the woods. "Pappy sometimes uses vines as rope to tie firewood bundles. Do ye have a knife?"

"Yes!" Kep rummaged through his haversack and pulled out a small knife. He shot a silent thank you to whomever, likely Mule, had packed it back at KRONOS.

He sprinted after Mary to the nearby woods where they yanked down long winding brown vines that climbed through the thick woods. Kep sliced them at the base with his knife.

They raced back to the bridge and set to work. "I'll be making a net to hold the box." Mary grabbed a bundle of vines. "You take the longest one and attach it to this side. We need to make sure the vines will be long enough to reach the other side and suspend the box of gunpowder underneath the middle of the bridge."

Moments later, Kep had loop-knotted one end of a vine to the edge of a plank. There was just enough space between the planks to wedge the vine between.

Mary tied vines around the wooden box, which oddly reminded Kep of how his mom wrapped ribbons around Christmas gifts.

Then Mary took the two glass bottles from the basket, handing one to Kep. "Pour the oil along the rope. We need to be creating a wick. And be quick about it."

Kep removed a cork from the bottle and drizzled oil along the rope and then what was left he poured on the vines, though wet vines wouldn't burn easily. Mary did the same with the vines she'd wrapped the wooden gunpowder box with. A strong fish-like odor filled the air as the oil dripped out of the bottles. Kep used his hand to rub the oil into the vines.

The wind kicked up even higher as they worked, blowing small groups of damp leaves off the sides of the bridge to float into the gully below.

Soon, the box was tethered between two long vines.

Kep crouched next to the gunpowder box now netted between the two long rope vines and slowly lowered the box, using the vine that was tied at one end to a plank.

The second vine dangling down from the box like a garden hose over the ravine.

He lowered the box the full length of the vine. The box was now suspended between the two vines. He swung the vine to force the dangling box under the bridge toward the other side.

Mary, laying flat on her stomach, tried to catch the loose end to pull it toward her.

Once.

Twice she failed to grab the loose end of the vine.

"You'd need to swing it toward me more," she said.

Kep gritted his teeth and nodded. There was a reason people used enormous caution around explosives. Even to the extent of wearing slippers instead of shoes in a fort's ammunition storage to avoid static electricity that can quickly lead to—kaboom!

Still. There was a job to be done.

"I need a branch," said Mary. "A long one to hook the dangling end and pull it to my side."

Mary scrambled off the bridge and into the woods. Kep nervously glanced in the direction that Parr would be coming from.

Mary returned carrying a long branch. She flopped back on her stomach and held the branch ready.

Kep once again swung the vine toward her. This time her branch, with all its twigs, twirled and wrapped the dangling vine hanging from the other end of the box.

He rushed to her side of the bridge and they carefully pulled the branch, now entangled with the vine, toward them.

Kep barely breathed as they reeled in the vine with the caution of a fisherman with a prize catch.

They hauled the branch close enough to free the vine and then looped it around the plank on this side of the bridge.

Now the box hung directly under the bridge.

Teamwork!

"The explosion will be in honor of me brother." Mary surveyed the soon to be destroyed bridge. "I'd only be regretting we could not blow it up with those butchers on it!"

Chapter 27

Lost Hope

The wind grew stronger and tree branches thrashed on both sides of the bridge. Overhead skinny clouds skittered across the sky casting dark, flickering shadows.

Kep crouched beside the rope soaked in oil that led to the gunpowder box. Lighting the wick leading to the gunpowder box suspended below the bridge was the final step.

He dug inside his haversack for his small metal tinder box determined to complete his mission.

He dug further into the haversack, but still didn't feel the metal box. His heart beat faster. Its contents—a steel striker, flint, and char cloth— were key to lighting the wick.

Failure wasn't an option.

He dumped the contents onto the bridge.

There.

An enormous sense of relief flooded him.

He snatched the metal box from under the compass, maps, and other items.

"Get off the bridge," he told Mary. "I'll run for it as soon as the wick is lit."

She nodded and raced off the bridge.

He gripped the metal box. The final step. A whoosh of accomplishment ran through him as he lifted the box's lid.

A terrible, terrible mistake.

A gust of wind wafted the small black piece of cloth, the char cloth, loose from the box. Kep lurched to catch it, but it twirled and twisted across the bridge.

Horrified, Kep watched their only hope of starting a fire disappear to the gully below. The flint and striker were useless without that cloth.

A cold dread hollowed his insides.

"Kep, hurry and light it!" Mary called from the darkness.

"The char cloth—" Kep could barely get the words out "—blew away."

"No!" Mary's voice sounded shrill. "It mustn't all be for naught!"

Hoofbeats sounded. Muffled, but coming swiftly from the direction of the British camp.

A few damp leaves plastered the bridge planks. Kep plucked the driest one he could find.

He had one last hope. Maybe a leaf could serve as tinder.

Holding the metal striker in one hand, he sliced it against the flint. Tiny sparks landed on the dampish leaf.

He blew on it, hoping, praying for glowing embers.

Nothing.

The hoofbeats sounded nearer.

Fear prickled his skin.

Hands shaking, he tried again. Another spark. But the leaf didn't take it up.

"The leaves are too damp to light," Kep called to Mary.

Parr and his men would cross the bridge.

They would find Jacques.

And the letter!

Nathan Hale

When General George Washington needed a volunteer for an extremely dangerous spy mission, Captain Nathan Hale of the Continental Army volunteered.

Disguised as a schoolteacher, Hale slipped behind British lines on Long Island and successfully gathered information about British troop movements.

Hale was captured while trying to cross back into American-controlled territory. When incriminating documents were found on him, British General William Howe ordered his execution for spying.

The next morning at the gallows, legend holds that Hale was asked if he had any last words and that he replied with these now-famous words, "I only regret that I have but one life to lose for my country."

MISSION NOTES CORPS OF KRONOS

Chapter 28

Kaboom

"**K**ep!" Mary dashed across the bridge holding something toward him. "Moss. It's only a wee bit but drier than the leaves." Mary's dress flapped around her ankles in a wind gust. "We are not beaten yet!"

Kep grasped some of the feather-light material and shoved it into the tinderbox.

Men's voices could be heard, too far to hear the exact words, but close enough to send shivers down Kep's spine.

He couldn't fumble this!

Concentrating his energy to steady his hand, he held a bit of dry moss to the flint as he sliced the striker. The movement produced sparks that landed on the moss.

He blew gingerly.

And held his breath as embers glowed.

Mary added extra moss and soon a tiny flame burned bright.

The charred, acrid scent filled his nostrils and jubilation coursed through him.

Success.

Kep held the flame to the oil-soaked wick. Within seconds, fire sizzled slowly along it, creating a blazing snake headed directly to the powder box suspended underneath.

"Run!" Mary hissed.

Kep and Mary sprinted off the bridge and hid in the thick shrubbery.

From the opposite side of the bridge, hoofbeats sounded closer. Within moments, the shadowy figures of a band of men appeared around the bend of the road, riding at a fast gallop.

Parr and his men.

Closer.

Closer.

Kep anxiously stared at the bridge as the skinny rope of fire traveled too slowly.

The men were almost to the bridge.

The crackling, searing snake of fire grew more intense.

And then ...

Kaboom!

The center of the bridge exploded in a rain of wood pieces and sparks.

The soldiers' horses reared and shied violently.

Parr, outlined by the bright blaze, shouted at his men. "Fall back!"

Black smoke billowed as the bridge became an enormous bonfire.

Take that, you blasted British!" Mary uttered in a low voice.

Soon the smoke was so thick it was impossible to see across the bridge.

But one thing was certain.

There would be no crossing.

"Saboteurs!" yelled a voice in the dark. "Keep your guns out!"

"Return to camp!" Parr shouted.

The sound of retreating hoofbeats followed, perhaps the sweetest sound in the world.

"We did it!" Kep grinned so wide it felt his face might crack.

"The saints themselves must've been aiding us!" Mary said.

Parr and his bullies would not terrorize the Bannekers. They would not capture Jacques. They would not stop Burgoyne's secret letter from reaching General Gates.

"We make a great team!" Kep said.

"Indeed. And next, by God's teeth, we will be getting Finn out!" Mary said fiercely.

"We will." Breaking Finn out of jail was going to be a dangerous and difficult mission. But he and Mary would have Max, TJ, and Tela beside them.

For now, it was time to savor success.

Kep had come to 1777 Saratoga to determine whether Fox had tampered with history. And he'd found the answer was a dangerous yes.

But with the help of the Bannekers, Jacques, and Mary, they'd discovered the secret plot and Jacques should be on his way to warn American General Gates. While the impending arrival of a second British army, General St. Ledger's troops, still created a threat to democracy, American General Gates would no longer be at risk of a surprise attack. He could prepare.

They started back toward the Banneker's farm, their spirits high.

King of England

Early in 1776, King George agreed to hire thousands of Hessian mercenaries to assist the British troops already in America. He is quoted as saying: "The die is now cast; the colonies must either submit or triumph.... we must not retreat."

Known as Mad King George, George III ascended to the throne at age 22. His first attack of mental instability occurred in 1765 and after 1788 the attacks escalated. The brutal "treatments" included straitjackets and arsenic, which only made the symptoms worse. By 1811 George could no longer rule and his son George IV became prince regent, but soon afterward began to suffer some of the same afflictions as his father.

George III

Chapter 29

Goodbyes

A cart pulled by two enormous dogs jolted toward them along the rutted road.

Juba drove the cart, her chin high. Her grandparents sat in the back, their gray-haired heads close together. The powerful dogs loped along, pulling against their leather harnesses.

Jacques was not with them, a hopeful sign that he was now on his way to the Americans.

Juba stopped the cart. "We heard an explosion!"

"We couldn't be getting the beams to burn, so we blew it up." Mary threw her shoulders back. "No one saw us, and Parr's gang hightailed it back to camp like the cowardly curs they are."

"A strike in the fight for liberty," said Mr. Banneker.

"Jacques got away?" Kep asked nervously. "Your son brought the horse?"

"Yes." Mr. Banneker slid off the back of the cart. "My son will send up three shots to let us know when the letter is with General Arnold."

"Wait! I thought it was going to General Gates?"

"General Arnold will get it to him. The point is, we'll hear the shots when the letter is safely in the American camp."

Kep couldn't wait to hear those three shots.

Juba climbed down from the driver's seat. "I wanted to help with the bridge." She sounded disappointed.

Mary gently squeezed Juba's shoulder. "Ye have already helped. How would the letter have ever gotten to the Americans without you driving your cart? Ye'd be a wee one, but very brave."

"My pa says this is all our war," Juba said fiercely. "If we're to be free, we all need to fight."

Mrs. Banneker turned to Mary. "Would you like to stay with our family tonight?"

"I cannot," Mary said. "I must be getting back—somewhere."

Kep stared at her. "Somewhere" had to be the British camp.

"Can you give us a minute?" Kep pulled Mary aside.

"You can't go back to camp tonight!" Kep hissed.

"I'd not be leaving me brother in such times of trouble," she said simply.

Kep could understand that. But it would make planning Finn's escape much harder if they couldn't meet up outside the British camp first to coordinate. And for that, he needed to travel back to the modern world and get Max, Tela and TJ. Besides she was sooty and messy and if she arrived back at camp in that state the British might well suspect her.

"Stay with the Bannekers at least until tomorrow. I'll be back then. With more help." Kep didn't know exactly how KRONOS sent him places in time. But once Annie learned that Finn was in trouble, she'd make sure his team got back ASAP.

"Where would ye be going?" she looked at him sharply.

"To get us more help to save Finn. Stay with the Bannekers," Kep urged again. "You can't help Finn tonight. Working out the logistics together, as a *team*, before you go back will improve our success odds."

She frowned, unconvinced.

"You've still got your pass," Kep said. "And the story about your ill aunt. They won't expect you back this soon. Just give me until tomorrow. Please."

Much to Kep's relief, Mary finally agreed.

Kep glanced up at the starry night sky. Long past time to leave 1777.

Kep and Mary walked back to where the Banneker's waited by the cart.

"Thanks for all you did and all the risks your son took to get that letter to General Gates," Kep said to Mr. and Mrs. Banneker.

"Freedom never comes without sacrifice." Mr. Banneker held out his hand and shook Kep's in a grip surprisingly strong for an eighty-year-old. "That word is sweetest perhaps to those who have lived deprived of it."

Kep squatted down next to Juba to say goodbye. Her dogs kept a steady watch. "You and Liberty and Patriot make a pretty impressive team."

"Promise I get to help if you blow up any more bridges," Juba insisted.

"I suspect you'll help with future adventures," Kep said. "You're a total boss girl."

Juba grinned, seeming to understand the centuries-out-of-place phrase.

Mary told the Bannekers she had changed her mind and would be staying with them after all. Then she squeezed Kep's hand. "Don't tarry on returning. Do you have a long journey ahead?"

"Long enough." Kep hoisted his haversack higher on his shoulder. "I'll be back with some familiar faces."

"You're leaving? You know you're welcome to stay with us too," offered Mrs. Banneker.

"Indeed," said Mr. Banneker. "You've done such a good job here, we could use your help on a new problem that I've just learned about."

Kep doubted he had the bandwidth to add much more in the problem arena, but also wanted to help this amazing family any way he could. "What's the problem?"

Mr. Banneker grimaced. "My son told me there's word the local Loyalists have captured all the ammunition supply wagons headed to the American camp."

"*What*?" Kep's mind flashed to the letter. On October 7th we'll make our attack. "That would be a disaster!"

"We're turning over every leaf in the countryside," said Mr. Banneker. "We could use another pair of sharp eyes."

Kep blew out a breath. Problems never end. "I have to go now, but I'll be back as quickly as I can. And I'll bring some extra pairs of sharp eyes for the hunt."

Mr. Banneker nodded. "Missions remain, but our job tonight was critical. Remember that. No one action wins a war. It's an accumulation of brave acts by ordinary men and women asked to be great."

Mr. Banneker was right. Freedom had many costs. Americans had paid that price throughout the revolution and would continue to pay far into the future. No one person had won the War of Independence. Not even the great George Washington. Instead, countless Americans who would never appear in the history books had stood together defending liberty against those who would threaten its existence.

"We should check real quick to make sure that fire hasn't spread. With the dampness, it's doubtful, but we'll give it a glance over," said Mrs. Banneker.

"I better get going." Kep looked around at the faces gathered. The brave and the bold. He vowed to help them, help the cause with all he had.

Then he jogged away.

He was still running in the direction of the transport when three sharp rifle cracks broke the quiet of the night.

He raised his fist toward the sky. Jacques had delivered the letter to the American camp.

Spy Messages

Both the British and Continental armies employed spies to gather information about troop numbers, weapons, supplies and intended plans to march or attack. Loyalist sympathizers often gave the British army details about the geography and terrain, which were unfamiliar to the British army.

Washington recognized the importance of counterintelligence and placed his spies behind enemy lines. But he was also the victim of fake intelligence coming from British agents and loyalist sympathizers.

Secret messages and battle plans were passed in many creative ways, including being sewn into buttons, written in code, written with invisible ink, or written as mask letters. A mask letter could only be read by placing a unique cut out shape over the written letter. The words visible after placing the shape over the writing would be the secret message.

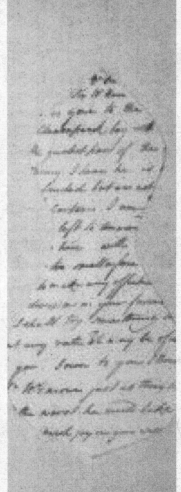

Mask Letter

Chapter 30

Return Home

Kep slowed when he saw the tall aspen he'd used as a landmark and made his way to the transport site. There, he pushed aside the stacked branches to access the tunnel. Once inside, he carefully tugged them back into place to shield the opening.

He made his way back through the cave to the wall, found the button, and the door slid open.

One he got inside the transport, control panels flickered all around him. When he adjusted his headset, a familiar voice crackled.

"What is the update on Fox?" Annie got right to the point.

Nothing like: I'm glad you're alive, nephew.

"Fox was here. He created a secret plan with Burgoyne to flank General Gates with a second army. But now it's not going to be a surprise attack."

"Well done."

"But there are other problems. The Loyalists have stolen the ammunition supply wagons headed to the American camp." Kep took a deep breath. "And Finn has been arrested by the British. He—he could be executed within days."

Silence.

Annie probably needed a minute to process this information considering she, like Kep, would cease to exist if Finn died in 1777.

"We'll need to come back. ASAP," Kep continued. "Emphasis on *we*. Let the team know."

"Roger that," Annie said with the slightest croak to her voice.

The transport engines vibrated to life He clicked safety restraints into place and prepared to depart Saratoga, 1777.

He'd be back.

A car with black tinted windows pulled into the school parking lot. It was 2 a.m. Kep, his hair still damp from a shower at the transport center, back in a sweatshirt, with his swim bag instead of a haversack, sat exhausted in the back seat. His driver, Mule, had kindly refrained from asking a thousand questions about the mission.

Under a streetlight, his bike waited in the bike rack.

Mule turned to Kep. "Heard you're going back. With your team."

"Yeah, maybe I sort of overestimated what I could do by myself. But I created a new team in 1777."

"Toning down that maverick streak of yours is an important lesson," Mule said.

"I think it's one Finn McGee could learn," Kep muttered.

"Anyway, it sounds like you did a good job at Saratoga."

"Thanks," Kep said. "Hey, were you the one who packed my haversack?"

"Yep."

"The hunting knife you put in there may have saved history."

Mule tipped his cowboy hat. "Glad to play a role. Toss your bike in the trunk and I'll drop you a block from home."

Kep shook his head. "It's just a ten-minute ride. It'll feel good to clear my head."

"I'll follow you then. Just to make sure you get home safe."

Kep climbed out of the car and strode toward the bike rack. The scent of freshly mowed grass and the distant hum of traffic filled the air.

Modern American life.

He glanced up at the American flag in the school's courtyard. A cool, bright spotlight shone on the stars and stripes. He thought of General Burgoyne and his officers, so confident that the king's soldiers would soon bring the Americans to their knees. He thought of the rebels gathered at General Gates camp. Preparing for the British attack. Preparing to defend the idea of freedom.

The rebels had to win. America itself hung in the balance of the outcome of the Second Battle of Saratoga.

Headlights followed him as he rode his bike along the sidewalks.

At home, the house was mostly dark. Light spilled from only two rooms: the kitchen and Max's room.

Mule rolled down the window. "See you soon, kid."

The sedan sped away and Kep wheeled his bike into the garage. At the back door, Piper met him with a happy bark, her tail wagging a hundred miles an hour.

He rubbed her favorite spot behind her ears. "I met some pretty impressive canines on this trip. But you're still top dog to me."

The empty kitchen smelled like freshly baked cookies. Neatly stacked plates, glasses, and cereal bowls dried in the strainer next to the sink, ready for a new day. His mom had left a bright pink post-it note on the table next to a plate of peanut butter and jelly sandwiches and chocolate chip cookies. "I hope the swim meet was a success!"

Kep's stomach growled. He couldn't remember his last meal.

He found a pitcher of lemonade in the fridge, poured a glass, and sat down at the table. Before he took his first bite, footsteps sounded on the stairs.

His little brother appeared in the kitchen doorway. He wore a pair of Kep's hand-me-down pajamas, oversized on his skinny frame, and a fierce scowl. "You went without me. Didn't even tell any of us. I thought we were a team."

So Annie had already contacted his brother, and probably TJ and Tela as well.

"Sorry." Kep sighed. "I thought I could do it all myself. I was a little cocky."

"A *little*?" Behind his glasses, Max rolled his eyes.

"It won't happen again." Even as he said those words, he knew it was more complicated than just being cocky. He wanted his little brother, his friends, his family safe. In that sense he was no different than Mary trying to protect Finn or Juba's grandparents trying to defend their family.

And that wasn't going to change. But he'd also realized trying to do everything by yourself can make things even more dangerous for the people you care about, the very people you're trying to protect.

"Did you win your chess tournament?" he asked.

"Obviously." Max nudged his glasses up, came into the kitchen, and took the chair opposite Kep. "And don't change the subject."

"We're going back there, to 1777 Saratoga," Kep said. "All of us."

"I know. Annie sent a text." Max looked a little too eager at the prospect. He helped himself to a handful of cookies. "What're we going to do?"

"Save America."

"Some specifics would help. Start with what happened on your one-man-band mission."

"There was a secret letter. It had to get to American General Gates." Kep got up to grab a second glass from the cupboard, filled it with lemonade, and handed it to his brother.

Between bites of his sandwich, Kep filled Max in on the adventure.

"You know what's weird?" Max said slowly.

"What part *isn't*?"

"That note from Burgoyne. That it wasn't in code. Or secret ink. Or some kind of mask letter."

"And?"

"It's almost like he wanted it to be found, to be read."

"Meaning?"

"I think there's something more to the story. Some deeper plot."

Kep had an uneasy feeling. "I guess we'll find out when we get back." He held out the plate of cookies. "By the way, we'll also need to help our old friend Finn escape from the British camp."

"Finn? Finn McGee?" Max's eyes popped wide. "From Boston?"

"Grab some more cookies. It's a long story."

THE END

Let's connect!

 @Eileen_Schnabel

@eileenschnabelauthor

@eileenschnabelauthor

@eileenschnabel

Pinterest

not chpt. 28?

About The Author

Eileen Schnabel had taught law for ten years when she wandered into a local cemetery and spotted the grave of a soldier who'd served under George Washington. Thinking of the hardships of Valley Forge and the sacrifices of those early soldiers, she wondered if modern Americans still had the grit to fight the Revolutionary War. To answer that question, she sent four kids back in time to Boston, 1775, to take Paul Revere's midnight ride, hang the famous lanterns at Old North Church, and rescue John Hancock and Samuel Adams from hanging as traitors to the crown.

Eileen's husband and two sons were eager to take on the time-travel adventure, but she insisted they remain in the twenty-first century. For now, the family lives in Wisconsin with their Goldendoodle, Piper, but something that looks like a time machine is taking form in their basement, so stay tuned for future books.

Eileen has an MA in journalism from Stanford University and a JD from the University of Iowa. You can find out more at www.eileenschnabel.com.

Additional Resources

BOOKS

Fiction:

Chains by Laurie Halse Anderson

Nonfiction:

Black Heroes of the American Revolution by Burke Davis

The American Revolution Great Battles For Boys by Joe Giorello.

INTERNET

The National Parks has an online tour of the battle of Saratoga:
https://www.nps.gov/sara/learn/photosmultimedia/virtual-tour-start.htm

Museum of the American Revolution
https://www.amrevmuseum.org/learn-and-explore/for-students-and-educators/resources-opportunities-for-educators/mini-lesson-plans

THE AMERICAN BATTLEFIELD TRUST
https://www.battlefields.org/visit/battlefields/saratoga-battlefield

History.com
https://www.history.com/topics/american-revolution/battle-of-saratoga

For additional resources, visit: www.eileenschnabel.com

Made in the USA
Monee, IL
11 January 2023

25048743R00122